# The G Girls

## *A Frenemy Who-Dunnit*

## S J Valentine

**Dragicorn Press**

# CONTENTS

# DEAR READER

The main characters in *The G Girls* were invented by me, the author. You may like them. You may not. I introduce them to you in the first chapter and, I confess, I find them a little icky. So, even if you don't like them after the first chapter, I encourage you to keep reading. You may feel differently about them by the end of the book. And even if you don't, it doesn't matter. I think there is value in their story whether you like the characters or not. None of us are so perfect that we cannot benefit from another's story, even if it is just to decide that is not who we want to be.

S. J. Valentine

"It takes a great deal of bravery to stand up to your enemies, but a great deal more to stand up to your friends."

- Dumbledore

*(from Harry Potter and the Sorcerer's Stone)*

ΔΔΔ

*No animals were harmed in the writing
of this book but a few of them may
have had their feelings hurt.*

# SATURDAY NIGHT

## CHAPTER 1

Juliette Lyons gathered up her long black hair, twisted it into one thick strand, and pulled it over her shoulder. She leaned back against the wooden bleachers of the Deerfield High School gym. Flanked by four other girls, Juliette lounged like Queen Cleopatra surrounded by her ladies-in-waiting.

The little group sat by themselves on the bleachers while a crowd of kids pushed in towards the center of the gym. Julie peered passively into the crowd amassed on the gym floor. She patiently waited for the commotion to die down, knowing that the attention would eventually turn back to her.

From the middle of the gym floor, Darlene Blaise caught sight of Julie and her entourage sitting by themselves on the bleachers.

*What is she doing way over there?* Dar wondered.

She immediately realized the answer to her own question: Juliette Lyons would never be jammed into anonymity in a crowd of kids, especially not a crowd of kids all focused on someone other than her.

Dar knew she should go sit with Julie, but she did not budge. Instead, she turned her attention back towards the center of the crowd, raising herself up on her tippy-toes and craning her neck to see if she could make out what was going on.

△△△

Fifteen minutes ago, Dar was out on the gym dance floor, dancing with her friend Robert Ferrier. Julie had nicknamed him "The Ferret." "I find it hard to believe that I'm the only person who calls him that," Julie had said after Dar had admonished her to "be nice."

Robert was a bit of a gork (geek + dork), but Dar didn't mind. She wanted to dance, so while her friends were preoccupied with the bunch of bros (bro-zzos, bro-tozoa, bro-mides, bro-pes) that had been competing for their attention all evening, Dar slipped off to dance with Robert.

They were on the dance floor for only a few minutes when suddenly, a wall of kids almost knocked them over. It was then that Dar became aware of shouting, punctuated by screams from some of the girls. The music stopped abruptly. She turned to see what was going on, but the crowd had already condensed into a tight knot, blocking her view. Seconds later, the teachers were in motion, pushing their way through the crowd. The police followed shortly after.

Dar was well on the outskirts of the crowd, and although she was 5'7," she soon realized she was not going to be able to see a thing. Robert had disappeared, no doubt swept away by the collective force of kids pushing and shoving. The only sound she could hear was the muffled buzz of people talking in subdued tones. Whatever had happened was essentially over. Reluctantly, Dar turned away from the crowd and headed towards Julie.

"Why do you dance with him?" Julie asked as Dar approached her. Julie barely glanced in Dar's direction before turning her eyes back towards the center of the room.

"He's harmless," Dar replied, taking her place beside Julie. She was not interested in discussing whether she should dance with Robert. Dar had wanted to dance, and she did exactly what she had wanted to do. It was none of Julie's business, and besides, Robert was really sweet.

Robert was in Dar's Algebra II class. They sat near each other and frequently worked on homework problems together. Robert was easy to talk to, even if he was a bit awkward. When he asked Dar to dance, she knew it was not out of any serious interest in her. Robert was completely gone over a girl named Sara Schaeffer. Practically the whole sophomore class knew that. Everyone except Sara, of course.

"I know he's harmless. He's the sidekick," Julie snapped. "'The Ferret' is the perfect name for him."

Dar felt herself break into a half smile at this. Robert's long, angular features, curly cropped black hair, and intense dark eyes did not immediately call to mind the image of a ferret, but once Julie had given him the nickname, it was easy to imagine him as the beady-eyed little creature.

Dar glanced at Julie. She was looking straight ahead slightly smiling. When she caught sight of Dar's nearly imperceptible movement in her direction, she broke into a full smile, and the two of them sat there together grinning, eyes trained on the center of the room.

Dar had come to the dance that evening with her best friends: Juliette Lyons, Ariel McAllister, and Daniella Lucci. Around school they were known as "the Gorgy Girls." The appellation was meant to be derogatory as in, "they think they're so *gorge*." It was usually accompanied by an eye-roll, or a knowing exchange of glances. Nonetheless, Julie embraced the name.

"What's wrong with being called 'gorgy'?" she asked. "From now on we will be '*the G Girls*'; 'G' for 'goooorgeeeous,'" she proclaimed, tossing her head back and pushing her hair up on her head for emphasis.

"I guess it's better than being called 'the *F Girls*'," Dar responded. They all looked at her with surprise.

"'F' for 'faaaabulous'," she said, mimicking Julie's head and hair gestures. "What did you think I meant?"

So that's what they called themselves: *the G Girls*. They had other friends too, and they were often included in a wider social network. Yet the four of them banded together and were nearly inseparable.

Dar was secretly proud to be part of this group. She knew that she and her friends were really sic. They were the school influencers - the 'A' list. Other girls looked upon them with a mixture of envy and intimidation. Guys followed them around like dogs on a leash, and even though they were only sophomores, everyone in school knew who they were.

$$\triangle\triangle\triangle$$

Out on the dance floor, the noise was increasing. People were starting to talk at a normal volume again. The crowd was breaking up and spreading out.

One of the frosh girls was making a beeline for Dar and Julie, eager to be the one to tell the *G Girls* just exactly what the commotion had been about.

Dar, Julie, and the rest of the girls turned their attention expectantly in the direction of the approaching frosh as if they had sent her out as a scout and were now patiently awaiting her return.

"Girl fight," the frosh said excitedly. "It was Carrie Ellis and Teresa Manning. The police arrested them. Handcuffed them and everything."

Dar felt her mouth drop open. *Carrie Ellis? Arrested?*

There was a moment of silent shock and surprise before all the girls began plying the beaming frosh with questions - all except Julie. She continued to look coolly in the direction of the fawning little messenger. And Dar thought she noticed the subtle look of satisfaction in Juliette's deep blue eyes and an almost imperceptible smile just at the corners of her lovely pink lips.

# MONDAY
## CHAPTER 2

On Monday morning, the entire student body was circulating photos and videos of the Ellis-Manning fight. A non-stop procession of pics and vids passed from phone to phone all morning long. There were videos of kids on the dance floor before the fight; videos that captured the sounds of the fight from various positions in the crowd; and videos that showed Carrie Ellis and Teresa Manning being taken away by the police.

There were also a few videos of the fight itself. These showed a blurry collage of intertwined body parts belonging to Teresa Manning and Carrie Ellis. The videos were short and chaotic due to bystanders getting in the way. They captured snippets of the action, but no one was able to get clear footage of the entire fight from start to finish.

The photos and videos provided much enjoyment for the student body throughout most of the morning. At first kids were just passing them around, but soon they began adding their own comments and memes. The photos took on captions. The funniest among these moved through the school like a hoard of Tasmanian devils, spinning out little dust storms of amusement as they went.

By the afternoon, everyone had seen the images; everyone had read the jokes; everyone had exhausted their own reservoir of one-liners. The topic was done. Everyone moved on.

Dar, Julie, Ariel, and Danni planned to go to Julie's house after school. Julie recruited her brother's friend Sean to give them a ride.

The girls caught up with Julie in the hall after the last bell. They followed her out of the building and towards the parking lot. They could see Sean in the distance. He was leaning up against a large white car, waiting for them. His butt was against the oversized vehicle, and his head was angled downward. He had an earbud in his ear and was clearly listening to some music while he tapped the ground with a sneaker-clad foot. He was holding what looked like a big bag of gummy bears in his hand. Periodically, he would put a candy into his mouth. In between smacks and chews, he would sing a few lines of the song he was listening to.

As the girls approached him, Julie took off running like a sprinter. She ran straight at Sean, making a grab for his candy. Sean was too quick for her, though. He must have caught sight of her coming from the corner of his eye. He quickly thrust his hand up above his head, just out of Julie's reach. She leapt up into the air and came down with a loud *splat*, overshooting her target. She turned around and tried again, but Sean kept the bag up over his head while moving slightly out of her way. They danced around like this for a second or two, eyes locked on each other. Then, Julie gave up.

"Share," she demanded, holding out her hand.

"How about 'please,' " Sean suggested in a disgusted tone.

"Pa-leeeaze," Julie said, exaggerating the word.

Sean shook a few gummies from the bag into her hand. By then, Dar, Ariel, and Danni had arrived, also holding out their hands. Sean shook a few gummies from the bag into each of the girls' hands.

"Thank you, Sean."

"Thank you, Sean."

"Thank you, Sean," the girls chorused.

Sean closed the bag. He opened the car door and got in. The girls followed his lead, with Julie in the front seat; Dar, Ariel, and Danni in the back seats.

As soon as they were strapped in and underway, Julie peaked her head around the back of her seat.

"So, Carrie Ellis and Teresa Manning," Julie began, "how juvie to get into a fight at the school dance!"

"They've both been suspended for three weeks," Ariel said matter-of-factly as she sucked on one of her gummy bears. "Because of the fight," she added as if no one knew why.

"Really, where did you hear that?" Danni asked. "I thought it was only two weeks."

"Three weeks. Because of the zero-tolerance policy."

Ariel moved the gummy bear around in her mouth and swallowed before speaking again.

"I heard it from Megan Cushing. Her mother is friends with Mrs. Anderson, who works in the school office. Mrs. Anderson knows everything that goes on at DHS," she explained.

Julie picked up the bag of gummy bears that Sean had stashed in the cup holder between them. She opened the bag and shook out two candies for herself. Then, she offered the bag to Dar and Danni. Each took two more candies before handing the bag back to Julie.

"If you had to pick the least likely person to get into a fight and get suspended, wouldn't you pick Carrie Ellis?" Danni asked, popping one of her new gummies into her mouth.

"I know, right?" Ariel replied. "But actually, Teresa Manning told Cindy Farr that she was going to flatten Carrie's ass at the dance."

"Really?" the girls responded, turning to look at Ariel. This was new information.

"You mean Teresa Manning was actually *planning* to attack Carrie Ellis?" Danni asked. "What possible reason could Teresa Manning have for going after Carrie Ellis?"

"I can't imagine that Carrie ever did anything to Teresa. It's hard to believe that they even knew each other," Dar commented, rolling a gummy around in her mouth.

"Well, you know how beastie Teresa is," Ariel said. "She is scary. She isn't a person who needs a reason to attack anyone. Carrie probably just looked at Teresa the wrong way, or maybe Carrie sat at Teresa's favorite lunch table. She was probably just in the wrong place at the wrong time. That's all it takes with Scary Terry."

It was true that Teresa Manning was basically a thug. It was not unusual for her to threaten someone just for glancing at her. She attempted to intimidate and terrorize anyone who got in her way. And, she was big, at least 5'10" and 170 lbs.

A few months before, Teresa Manning punched a girl who had accidentally bumped into her in the hallway. She was suspended for that too, but no one was arrested. The incident had earned her the nickname "Scary Terry."

Carrie Ellis, on the other hand, was a quiet, straight "A" student. The closest she ever came to being violent was whacking a tennis ball with her racket. She was medium height, about 5'3," and very slender; not at all the type to get into a fight.

"Carrie was probably just an easy target," Sean offered. The girls all looked at him with surprise. They

11

hadn't expected him to speak.

"What?" he asked, "It's a known fact that bullies tend to target kids that are weak."

"But I really wouldn't call Carrie 'weak'," Dar said. "I mean, she's quiet, but she's not socially awkward."

"I agree," Ariel said. "She's not socially awkward. She's just basic and a little too good to be interesting."

"Well, Teresa fixed that," Danni observed. "We're finding her interesting now."

The girls giggled. There was a pause in the conversation. Then, Julie began again.

"I wonder who won?" she mused.

"Won?" Dar repeated dumbly.

"Won the fight, Dar," Julie said. "It's hard to tell what happened from the photos."

*Who won the fight? Sometimes Julie can be so harsh,* Dar thought.

However, when it came to Carrie Ellis, Dar knew the reason why; Julie was jealous of Carrie.

## ∆∆∆

Carrie Ellis was the girlfriend of Damon Johnston. Carrie and Damon had been together for about nine months. They appeared to be quite tight. They were an odd match: an ostentatious athlete who strutted around the halls of DHS and a quiet, studious, almost mousey girl who had just a few close friends. Still, they made a good pair and really seemed to care about each other.

However, before there was *Damon and Carrie*, there had been *Damon and Julie*. Damon and Julie started going out in May of 8th grade and split up just after the start of 9th grade – a total of five months.

Julie really liked Damon. She pursued him with every tactic she could think of. She flirted and teased and won his affections, but she had no idea how to maintain a relationship beyond the initial chase. She was moody and pouty and demanding. She continually created drama where there was no real need for it.

Julie craved Damon's constant attention. She became angry over the least little thing. If he went out with his friends, she sulked. If his attention wandered in the least, she got mad. And while some guys might enjoy the game, it wasn't Damon's style. If Damon's choice of Carrie showed anything, it was that Damon preferred a solid relationship with a girl who could be a good friend rather than a wild ride with an emo *G Girl* like Julie.

It was Damon who ended the relationship with Julie. But if Julie was crushed, she did not show it. She moved on quickly, resuming her role as queen of her entourage. However, Dar suspected that deep down inside, Julie was very, very hurt.

Dar stayed friends with Damon even after he and Julie split up. She did not see much of him during their frosh year, but this year they had study hall together. She shared a table in the library with Damon every Thursday. Dar kept this information from Julie, however, knowing that Julie would be upset if she knew.

Now Dar was curious to find out what had really happened on Saturday night. She wanted to know just how Carrie and Teresa had gotten into a fight. She was sure that Damon would be able to tell her the whole story, but she would have to wait until Thursday to talk to him.

As for Carrie Ellis, Dar consciously avoided her even though she felt no ill will towards Carrie. It was one thing for Dar to sit with Damon during study hall, but quite another for her to befriend the rival girlfriend.

$$\triangle\triangle\triangle$$

"Do you really think Carrie Ellis had a chance of taking Scary Terry?" Danni asked her friends.

"I doubt it. Terry is Terry-fy-ing. She's a club," Ariel said.

"She's a trog," Julie offered.

"She's a thal," Danni added.

"She's the missing link," Ariel smirked.

"Actually," Dar said slowly, "someone told me that Carrie broke Teresa's jaw. That's why she was arrested. That must have been a shock for Scary Terry. And now, Teresa's friends are going around threatening to do damage to Carrie's friends."

"*Tseeeeeeeeelllllll!*" Sean made a high-pitched whistling sound through his closed teeth.

"That girl is pure! I'm impressed!" he exclaimed.

"I don't believe it," Julie responded. "I don't believe Carrie Ellis would be able to hit anyone that hard, especially not Teresa Manning."

They pulled into Julie's driveway. Everyone got out of the car. Julie exited the front seat. She slammed the car door as if irritated by the notion that Carrie Ellis had successfully fought off Teresa Manning. But a second later, she was calm.

Sean headed towards the sliding glass doors of the basement where Julie's brother Jeff was waiting for him.

Just before he opened the door, Julie called out to him. "Thanks for the ride, Seannie," she said.

"Yeah, well, the fare for your own personal ride service is a game of pool. You all owe me," Sean replied. Then, he slid open the door and disappeared into the basement.

## △△△

Julie now turned to her friends. "My mother is home,'" she said.

All the girls groaned. Mrs. Lyons always insisted

that Julie and her friends greet her upon arriving home. This would not be so bad except for the fact that Julie's mother had a not-so-subtle habit of looking each of them up and down. They could actually see her eyes moving from their heads to their toes. It was a most uncomfortable feeling.

"Being examined by your mother is worse than walking in front of the entire football team," Ariel said. "Why doesn't she make your brother and his friends parade before her?"

"She tries, but Jeff just ignores her," Julie answered.

They proceeded into the house through the kitchen door. They deposited their backpacks and bookbags onto a bench. Julie headed to the refrigerator to pull out drinks.

"Julie, is that you?" her mother called.

"Yes," Julie replied.

"I'm out here in the sun room," Mrs. Lyons informed them.

"I'll be there in a minute. I've got Dar, Ariel, and Danni with me. We're just getting something to drink."

Julie distributed bottles of iced tea and water to each of the girls and took one for herself. Drinks in hand, they all traipsed off to greet Julie's mother.

They found Mrs. Lyons stretched out on a window seat basking in the sun, a laptop precariously balanced on her lap. She was gingerly typing away on the keyboard as she studied the screen. The family's cat, Bradley, snoozed beside her.

Once again, Dar was struck by how much Julie and her mother looked alike. Both were tall and muscular with long black hair and defined cheekbones. The major difference was that Mrs. Lyons' almond-shaped eyes were a striking hazel-green while Julie's eyes were big, round, and crystal-clear blue.

Mrs. Lyons finished typing. She closed the laptop. She turned her attention to the girls.

"Hi, Mom," Julie said as she entered the room. Julie crossed the room to where her mother was sitting to pet the cat.

"Hi, Mrs. Lyons," the girls echoed as they followed Julie into the room.

"Hi, girls," Mrs. Lyons responded. "What are you up to this afternoon?"

"We're going to play pool for a little while," Julie said.

Mrs. Lyons watched as her daughter leaned over to scratch Bradley's ears. The cat stretched and purred with pleasure. Then, she turned to look at each of the girls. There was an awkward moment of silence as she eyed each one of them.

"What about homework?" she asked finally.

"I'll do it after dinner. I don't have a lot," Julie said.

"'Sounds good," Mrs. Lyons replied.

Julie took that as her cue to leave. She stood up and began leading the group towards the door.

Mrs. Lyons watched as the girls exited the room. "Dar, I like your skirt," she called out.

"Thank you," Dar said, turning around as best as she could to address her.

As they were heading towards the basement, Julie said under her breath, "Dar, I'd burn that skirt if I were you."

ΔΔΔ

Juliette Lyons had one weird talent, if you could call it that. She had a knack for playing games - and winning them. She loved games. She played any kind of game you could think of. And whether it was a game of chance or a game of skill, she won. If you were playing a team sport, you always wanted her on your team. She was good at everything. And she had the best luck of anyone Dar knew.

Being the younger sibling of two older brothers, Julie insisted on being allowed to participate in whatever games her brothers were engaged in. Her brothers were brutally competitive; they challenged each other in everything they did. They let Julie play, but they did not let her win simply because she was younger and female. She fought back by becoming good at everything: basketball, soccer, pool, throwing a football, video games, card games, Frisbee, baseball; whatever her brothers played, she played. She was even ruthless at Sorry and Monopoly.

Julie's father collected old sports cars as a hobby. There were always at least two cars in various states of dissolution and repair in their three-car garage. When the boys spent time with their father working on cars, Julie refused to be left out. She learned how to change spark plugs, tires, oil filters, and air filters. She was able to buff out a dent or repair a scratch. She examined engines and diagnosed problems right along with her brothers. She knew more about engines than most men.

Julie's older brother, Jeff, was a senior at DHS, and her oldest brother, Matt, was away in his second year of college. On holidays, the three of them still had gaming marathons together. And on snow days, when it was just Jeff and Julie, they challenged each other at the pool table for hours. Or they massacred each other endlessly at the gaming consoles until one of them collapsed.

ΔΔΔ

The girls descended a dark staircase that emptied

into a short hallway leading to a large, comfortable, finished basement. At the far end of the basement was a gas fireplace with a hearth. To the left of the fireplace, a flat-screen TV was mounted on the wall. In front of the TV was a set of soft, overstuffed couches arranged in an L-shape. A wide and chunky coffee table was conveniently positioned within reach of both couches.

At the near end of the room was a gaming area outfitted with a variety of games and an indoor picnic table. A double-doored cabinet, mounted on the wall, contained cue sticks dangling from a rack in a less than orderly fashion.

In front of the cabinet, and surrounded by four tall, cushioned stools, stood a classic old pool table; hefty and with netted pockets. The table originally belonged to Julie's grandfather on her father's side. Three generations of Lyons children grew up playing on it. The green felt was unevenly worn and on the verge of needing repair. Years of battles, losses and triumphs, seemed to be recorded on its surface, easily making the pool table the most intimidating object in the room.

Dar viewed the pool table as if it were a suspicious object teleported to Earth by an alien species with evil motives. She could not understand its allure in the least. She had no personal relationship to the pool table, no feel for the game, and no real interest. She only understood that the pool table provided a reason to gather, to organize, and to interact with Jeff and his friends.

Even when she was recruited to play, Dar spent the majority of the game focused on her phone. She only paid attention when it was her turn. It never occurred to her that if she gave the game any thought, if she practiced or got Julie to help her with it, she might actually improve or enjoy it. She just didn't care.

The best thing about the pool table was the four rich, red, comfy, bowl-like swivel chairs that were positioned on its outskirts. They were of a very contemporary design. You could curl up in those chairs and listen to music to your heart's content.

At the moment, two of those four chairs were occupied by Jeff and Sean. The two boys sat facing each other swiveling back and forth, clearly discussing something unimportant.

As the girls entered the room, Sean casually swiveled around to look in Julie's direction. She headed directly for him.

"You owe me a game of pool," he said. "Are you ready to pay up? Guys against the girls. Let's go."

Julie walked to where Sean was seated. They locked eyes for a moment. Then, Julie said, "Are you sure you want to play against me, Sean?" she paused. "Wouldn't you rather play *with* me?"

She smiled. She fluidly turned away from him. She headed towards the wall-mounted cabinet to pick out a cue stick. She had a little smirk on her face.

Sean watched her as she walked away. He seemed

to be contemplating the offer. Then, with the agility of large cat, he sprang out of his chair.

"'Works for me," he said. "Jeff, you're on your own."

Jeff glanced in the direction of his sister with a mild look of disgust. Then, he slowly turned his attention towards his other choices for a partner.

Dar felt her body tighten. She did not want to be drawn into a game of pool - not that she was likely to be chosen. Fortunately for her, Danni volunteered.

"I'll be your partner, Jeff," Danni offered affably.

"Thanks, Danni," Jeff replied. Then, he added loudly, "Not cool, bruh!"

"Perfect! Cause all I want to do is chill on the couches," Ariel announced, voicing Dar's thoughts exactly.

Ariel wheeled around and headed towards the big couches. Dar followed her. Seconds later, they were both stretched out on a couch, drinks on the coffee table, heads together so that they could share their latest discoveries.

Ariel pulled up a video from the DHS dance that she wanted Dar to watch. Then, Dar sent Ariel a funny little meme of an actual mouse terrorizing an actual cat with the caption "Scary CARRIE." Then it was back to videos from the dance.

ΔΔΔ

Dar must have drifted off. She had put in a pair of earbuds and had surrounded herself with her favorite music, blocking out the sounds in the room. The couch was so warm and comfortable. It enveloped her. Without thinking, she closed her eyes. Moments later, she was asleep. Slowly, she became aware that she had been sleeping. *For how long?* she wondered. She anxiously opened her eyes.

The first thing she saw was a face looking directly down at her, a face she didn't know. Dar let out an undignified little yelp and quickly sat up.

"You scared me!" she said, disoriented and a little annoyed.

There was a moment of silence. The boy in front of her was completely unfazed. He continued to stare down at her, arms crossed, patiently waiting for her to regain her composure.

"I'm told that you are the worst pool player in this room," he said matter-of-factly.

Dar was not sure what to do with this statement. *Does he expect me to confirm this?* she wondered.

"Yup. That would be me," she replied, slightly irritated.

Dar was now looking directly into the face of a tall, slender boy with broad shoulders. He was definitely older than she was. He had a round face with medium brown hair, silky and straight, and cut to his ears. He had light brown eyes and soft, pouty lips. His skin was translucent with a few freckles dotting the bridge of his small nose.

*Oh damn, he's cute!* Dar thought. She wanted to be mad at him, whoever he was, but she just couldn't be. He was too cute!

He reached out his hand. Dar took it without thinking. He pulled her up off the couch and led her around the coffee table before letting go.

"Where are we going?" she asked.

"Oh, sorry, you're my partner for the next game of pool. I'm Marc," he said, putting his hand out to her once more.

Dar took his hand delicately and held it for a second. "Dar," she said.

His hand was warm and sweet to the touch. Dar felt her cheeks flush imperceptibly. She noticed how easily her hand fit into his. *Marc and Dar. Our names fit together too,* she thought involuntarily. The thought surprised her. *Where did that come from?* she wondered. *What am I saying?*

They circumambulated the couches, and made their way back to the gaming area. Dar saw that the group standing around the pool table had expanded to include Drew Long, another friend of Jeff's. Ariel was standing next to Drew. Obviously, she had been recruited to be his partner. They were all waiting for her. How long had she been asleep? She could only imagine the conversation they had had about her and her pool skills before Marc came to wake her up.

Marc motioned to Dar to follow him over to the

wall cabinet. He stopped and looked her up and down. "How tall are you?" he asked, reaching for a cue stick.

"It doesn't matter. They're all the same," Sean interjected.

Marc was indignant. "Wha?" he exclaimed. "How can she be expected to succeed if she doesn't have a pool stick that fits her?"

"Nobody told me I was supposed to have my own stick," Dar chimed in. "No wonder I'm no good at this game."

"Hey, hey, no negativity," Marc admonished her. He handed her a pool stick. "We're going to have to make this work even if our equipment is both literally and figuratively *off-the-rack*." He chortled at his own joke.

"How are we all going to play at once?" Danni asked. "I thought only two people or two teams could play."

"Um, well, we'll play one-pocket," Jeff replied. "Each team is assigned a corner pocket. Whoever has the most balls in their pocket at the end of the game wins. It's a very simple concept."

Jeff and Sean then proceeded to enter into an intense discussion over who should get which pocket. Jeff, Sean, and Julie all thought there was an advantage to having the far right corner pocket. None of them was willing to give it up. The discussion became heated. All the teams got involved with each team arguing for their own advantage. Dar really didn't care, so whenever Marc spoke or made a point, she followed it up with "yeah, that."

Eventually, it was decided by consensus that they would all play four games while keeping the same teams. After each game, they would rotate the pockets so that no team was unfairly advantaged or disadvantaged.

*Oh Lord! Four games! Marc may be cute, but I am not sure he's worth enduring four games of pool*, Dar thought.

"Well, that took forever," Ariel said. "And we still have to decide who goes first, and who gets which pocket first," she added.

"I know how to do this," Julie said. She produced a pair of dice.

"Each team will roll the dice. The highest number will go first and will also get the far right corner pocket. For each game, we will rotate clockwise. Whoever has the far right corner pocket will always go first. We'll assign the rest of the pockets according to the dice, with the second highest number taking the near right, the third highest number taking the near left, and lastly, the lowest number taking the far left. Guys will shoot first on the first game. Girls will shoot first on the second game. We'll continue to alternate."

"You burned way too many brain cells figuring that out," Drew told her.

"I know, right?" Ariel agreed. "Let's just do it."

Each team rolled the dice to see who would go first, but not before they negotiated the rules even for that. Finally, it was decided that each person on each team would roll one die and the combined total of both dice would be their score.

They all took turns rolling a die. Then, they added up their throws. The results were Julie and Sean first, of course, followed by Ariel and Drew, Dar and Marc, and lastly Danni and Jeff.

No sooner had Julie and Sean won the far right corner pocket than Julie proclaimed that because they had rolled the highest number on the dice, they should be allowed to choose whichever pocket they wanted.

"What? You're the one who negotiated these rules," Jeff said to his sister. "And now you want to change them? Why? In order to give you some advantage? Why would we let you do that?"

Julie smiled cautiously like someone who had just gotten caught playing a practical joke. "Well, as the winners of the dice roll, I think we should have the right to choose," she said.

"Oh no, no, no. Those were not the rules we agreed to, right guys?" Jeff asked, gearing up for a fight.

There was an uncomfortable pause in the conversation as everyone tried to figure out what was going on, and whether they wanted to get into the middle of a fray between the Lyons siblings. The girls held back, not wanting to challenge Julie on an issue they barely cared about, but the guys quickly picked sides.

"I agree with Julie. We should be allowed to choose," Sean said.

"Of course you do. You're on her team," Drew responded.

"Yeah," Marc agreed.

"But Jeff," Julie reasoned, "Sean and I will pick the near right corner pocket and go second, so that is going to benefit you. Instead of going last, you'll be going first."

Dar quickly calculated that if Julie won on this point, Dar's turn would come last. She would be shooting eighth. That would be fine with her. The game could very well be over by then and maybe she would not have to take a turn at all. Dar's lack of both talent and interest in pool had never bothered her in the past. But now, with Marc as her partner, she felt a little nervous. Four games just meant plenty of opportunity for humiliation. *This is not going to turn out well for me*, she thought.

"I'm with Julie on this," Dar said self-servingly.

Everyone looked at her in surprise. Marc gave her a dirty look.

"Nope. We play it the way we agreed to," Jeff said. And, with Jeff, Drew, and Marc banding together and holding firm, Julie had no choice but to acquiesce.

"Fine. Sean's gonna break, and then you'll wish you had gone first," Julie said threateningly.

## △△△

Sean racked up the pool balls and positioned them at the far end of the table while everyone watched. He put the cue ball in position, took aim, and executed the opening shot. The triangle of balls burst apart with a tactile explosion. And, just like magic, the 15-ball headed directly for the far right corner pocket. It disappeared noiselessly.

"Yeah, baby!" Sean exclaimed. He and Julie clasped hands as Sean passed by her to maneuver into position for his next shot.

Julie bounced the end of her cue stick lightly on her brother's shoulder a few times.

"How did you like that shot, Jeff?" she asked. "Sean, Jeff wants to see more just like that one," she answered for her brother.

Jeff stood calmly holding his cue stick between his two hands, the rubber end resting on the floor. Years of being taunted by his sister had taught him not to react to her.

"I am zinn, Jules," he said in a low, tepid voice. "Just wait. Danni and I are going to crush it."

Sean continued his turn. He was left with a clear and easy shot, and he took it. Not only did he make the shot, he also set up the next shot. Then, he put that one in too.

"Yeah, that's what I'm talking about, Jeff. You

should have taken the offer to go first when you had the chance," Julie said, rubbing it in.

But now, Sean was stuck. With the cue ball poorly placed, and no possible shot, he opted to send the cue ball down the table in a defensive move. He used the cue ball to block Drew's pocket, leaving Drew with no pathway to access the pocket. The room erupted with objections.

"You can't do that," Drew said.

"Of course I can," Sean countered.

"You have to legitimately try to make a shot; at least aim for another ball."

"No, I don't," Sean said. "It's called *deee-fence*."

"Yes, you do," Jeff addressed Sean. "You have to hit another ball, or at least aim for one. That's a standard rule in any game of pool."

*Oh good, another delay!* Dar thought. *At this rate, I may never have to shoot.*

"It's a standard rule in eight-ball, but do we know for sure that it applies to one-pocket?" Julie asked. "We have no certain knowledge of that specific rule in one-pocket."

Now Jeff was getting exasperated.

"C'mon Jules, you know damn well that rule applies to one-pocket. It applies to all pool games," he said to his sister.

"I don't know that," she said serenely, having now met her goal of irritating her brother. "Do you have any proof?"

"Yeah, Jeff, where's your proof?" Dar demanded. "Google it and let's see."

Julie looked at Dar with surprise. "What are you up to?" she asked Dar in a quiet, private voice.

"What do you mean?" Dar replied with feigned innocence.

"You don't care about the rules of pool," Julie said.

"Yes, I do. I think Jeff should prove the rule or forget about it," Dar said without looking directly at Julie.

Julie paused a moment. She eyed her friend with amusement and suspicion.

"She's stalling cause she doesn't want to have to shoot," Marc announced to the two of them, invading their private conversation.

Dar was completely taken aback. *How did he know that?* She wondered.

"Am I right?" Marc asked, raising an eyebrow and looking directly at Dar.

Julie broke into a big smile followed by a slight chuckle at Dar having been outed. Then, she refocused her attention on Jeff ,who was continuing with his argument.

"It's a rule. I know it's a rule. Jules knows it's a rule. I'm not Googling it," Jeff said defiantly.

Julie hesitated, assessing her position. "Yeah, it's a rule," she said finally. "Sean, redo the shot."

△△△

The game continued. One-pocket turned out to be a difficult form of billiards because each team had only one pocket to work with and it was hard to get the shots to line up. Nonetheless, Drew and Marc were able to pocket one ball each.

Jeff managed to pocket two balls. But on his third try, he miscalculated. Not only did he miss the shot, he watched helplessly as the cue ball rolled down the table, coming to a stop perfectly positioned for his sister to take over.

"Nooooo!" Jeff cried amidst exclamations from everyone else.

Now, it was Julie's turn. She hopped off her stool. She did not smirk. She did not gloat over her brother's mistake. When it came right down to it, Julie took her games of pool seriously. And, she did not take any shot for granted, no matter how easy it looked.

Julie studied the table as she absent-mindedly chalked the tip of her cue stick. Then, she seamlessly glided into position to take her turn.

Julie executed her first shot with her mind focused on her next move. She did not even watch to make sure that the ball went into the pocket. She already knew that it would. She waited patiently for the cue ball to roll back into place so that she could execute her second shot.

As soon as the cue ball stopped, Julie leaned over the table. It was clear that she had already planned her next move. She deftly placed her cue stick in her left hand and rested it on the green felt. She slid the stick smoothly through her fingers a few times. Then, *smack!* The cue ball hit the object ball hard and stopped dead in place. The object ball sailed straight down the table and into Julie and Sean's pocket.

The cue ball was now perfectly placed for Julie's next shot. The room got quiet. Everyone was watching. Again, Julie executed her shot. Again, she sank the object ball. And once more, she left the cue ball in position for her next move. The onlookers were riveted.

"Very smooth," Marc said admiringly.

"She is very good," Danni said. "You cannot deny her that."

Julie sank her next shot and stood up. "I'm stuck," she announced. "I'm going to have to try something complicated."

Julie studied the table, walking all the way around to the other side and back again. Then slowly, almost reluctantly, she lifted her cue stick into place, resting it in her left hand. She swiveled her body so that her left hip made contact with the pool table. She aimed the stick at the cue ball in the direction opposite her ultimate goal. She seemed to be aiming at nothing at all, a spot on the rail known only to her. Then cautiously, carefully, she drew back her stick, and after a few practice slides, she took the shot.

The cue ball dutifully headed towards the rail. It bounced off and changed direction. It was now aiming for a ball that was positioned at the near end of the table. It made solid contact with a satisfying *clack*, sending the target ball reeling just seven inches into a second ball. The second ball then headed straight down the table towards Julie and Sean's pocket.

Everyone was watching with anticipation to see if the second ball was going to reach its destination, but there was very little doubt about it. The ball rolled straight down the table towards its goal. And as it came closer, a long, slow, encouraging cheer began to emit from the onlookers. It started softly and built in volume as the ball approached the pocket, culminating in a polyphonic chorus of "Yes!" as the ball dropped over the edge and met its destiny.

"That was bolts," Sean said, once the commotion had died down.

Julie looked happy and satisfied.

"I really didn't think I could make that shot," she admitted.

There were now three balls plus the cue ball left on the pool table. Julie's next shot was lined up and ready to go. The little helper ball that had been left behind was now in position to go straight into the far right corner pocket. It was a relatively easy shot compared to Julie's last feat.

She took the shot without fanfare and pocketed the ball - an unceremonious encore to her previous accomplishment.

"There's really no point in completing the table," Jeff pointed out after Julie had sunk her sixth ball. "Even if Jules misses the next two, no one can catch up to her. And Sean," he added. "Let's just start the next game."

*Yes!* Dar thought. *Yes, yes, yes! I don't have to shoot! One game down; three to go. If Julie shoots before me every game, this is going to work out perfectly for me.*

As if reading her thoughts, Marc said, "I think we should change the rules, or the order, or something because if Julie's turn comes before the rest of the girls every time, they may never get a chance to shoot."

"That's okay. That's no problem," Dar and Danni jumped in quickly.

"What are you so afraid of?" Marc asked Dar. "Don't worry. I'll help you. You're my partner. I'm not going to let you mess up."

Dar laughed defiantly.

"Oh really?" she scoffed as she eyed Marc suspiciously.

"Yes. Really."

He smiled, not looking directly at her.

She continued to stare at him. Marc's words were

so caring and personal, almost sweet, yet extremely annoying.

*Does he think that I am so uncomfortable with myself that I need him to save me from a game of pool?*

As Dar contemplated Marc, she caught sight of Julie staring in their direction. She suddenly felt she should turn her attention back to the game, even though she really just wanted to talk to Marc.

Julie abruptly took control of the conversation, refocusing on the question at hand.

"Actually, the way the rotation is set up, eventually all the girls will shoot before me," Julie explained. "But we can change the order for this round," she said obligingly. "Let's shoot in reverse order: Danni, Dar, Ariel, and then me."

"Fine," Dar said, resigning herself to her fate.

"Darn," Danni added.

"You were going to shoot first either way," Julie said to Danni in exasperation.

"Fine then! I'll break."

Danni stood up and began looking for the triangle.

"What are we doing?" Jeff asked when he saw Danni in motion. He, Ariel, and Drew had entered into a side conversation and were not paying attention to the latest revision in procedure. Sean had gone off in search of some iced tea and was just now returning to the group.

"We're going to reverse the shooting order so that I go last," Julie explained. "Last among the girls, I mean."

Danni found the triangle. She used it to gather the pool balls together, rolling them around on the table. She collected the last few stragglers by hand and placed them inside their triangular pen. She handed the whole thing off to Jeff who positioned the pool balls at the far end of the pool table for her. Then, Jeff removed the triangle in one grand gesture.

The last few years of hanging around with Julie and the guys had taught Danni everything she needed to know in order to play a casual game of pool. She wasn't a bad player, but still, she felt insecure when she played. As a result, she did everything with a slow, deliberate hand, as if the act of slowing down and controlling her movements would compensate for her sense of inadequacy. And actually, it did because in slowing down, she developed her own style of play. Her movements were interesting to watch, both awkward and graceful at the same time. With her tawny skin, soft limbs, and messy dark hair piled on her head, she projected the image of sensual femininity as she moved about the pool table. She did not have Julie's beautiful, graceful, well-manicured fingers, but her hands did have the capable strength of a good baker or a proficient chef. You could imagine her in the kitchen kneading bread, tossing spaghetti, or removing trays of cookies from the oven with those hands.

Danni carefully placed the cue ball where she wanted it. She slowly moved her stick into position. She took her time lining up the shot. Finally, she let the stick make contact with the cue ball. Her cautious movements produced just enough force to separate the triangle of balls adequately, but nothing more than that. Even though there was a cluster of balls resting in the vicinity of her pocket, the break did not leave her with a clear follow-up shot.

Danni peered at the table with a worried look on her face. Jeff came to her side to help her analyze the situation.

"I think you should try for the 9-ball," he said. "Look." He walked over to the cluster of balls. "Aim right here," he said patiently. "You have to hit the cue ball on this angle." He showed her the path the cue ball needed to take by drawing an imaginary line with his finger on the felted table.

Danni saw her shot as soon as Jeff pointed it out. She leaned over to take it but quickly stood up again to have one more look at the whole picture.

"You're going to have to hit the cue ball hard," Jeff said, aware of Danni's slow, measured style.

She leaned over again. Bolstered by Jeff's directions, Danni aimed and took the shot. The cue ball obeyed her. It did what it was told. It hit the 9-ball just right and landed it in the corner pocket.

"Yes!" Danni and Jeff clasped hands momentarily. "Now what should I do?" she asked Jeff.

"Hmm. Yup, you have nothing. You'll have to try a combination shot," Jeff replied.

The cue ball had come to a stop in an awkward location in the center of the table. Even though Jeff showed Danni how to line up her next shot, the position of the cue ball made it nearly impossible to execute. Danni did her best, but the shot was beyond her abilities.

"Nice try," Jeff said comfortingly.

So now it was Dar's turn. Despite her surface bravado, she was nervous. She too moved slowly, but it was more out of a reluctance to shoot than any natural rhythm. In the past, she had always been relaxed when she played pool. No one had had any expectation of her skills, and neither had she. She had always dutifully taken her turn, but without care. And once in a while, she even managed to pocket a ball. But mostly she just enjoyed being part of the group rather than the game itself. Furthermore, she had developed an identity around being the *G Girl* who really could not play pool. But now, Marc was making such a big deal out of her doing well that she felt anxious.

Dar picked up a cue stick. She moved into the vicinity of the cue ball. She stood waiting.

"Okay, Coach Wannabee," she addressed Marc. "Here I am, ready for your brilliant guidance. Tell me what to do."

Marc came to her side. He surveyed the pool table.

"You actually have a pretty good shot," he said, pointing to the alignment of the cue ball and the 6-ball. "Just hit the cue ball right here along this path." He drew an imaginary line on the table just as Jeff had done for Danni.

Dar put the tip of the cue stick in her left hand. She began by placing her left hand on the table, bending over awkwardly. She took aim, sliding the pool stick back and forth between her fingers a few times.

"Wait! Stop!" Marc loudly interrupted her.

Startled, Dar abruptly jerked herself upright, tipping the cue ball in the process. The ball calmly spun off to the side. The room exploded in reaction.

"The cue ball moved. That's her turn. No do-overs," resounded from a chorus of voices.

Dar glared at Marc; her jaw tight, her lips pursed. She wanted him to know in no uncertain terms that she did not appreciate his uninvited interference.

"C'mon, guys." Marc rolled his eyes at the group. "You can't honestly count that as her turn."

"These are the rules," Sean said. "We don't make them up. Or, at least not that one."

"You're being ridiculous. If Dar is supposedly so bad, why are you all afraid of giving her a second chance?" Marc continued.

"I must be a threat to them, Marc," Dar said nonchalantly.

"Yeah. They know if they give you the opportunity,

you'll dominate the game," Marc responded.

Jeff drew in a deep breath and let it out. "Okay, let her take the do-over," he relented.

"I'm still annoyed with you," Dar told Marc as she once again prepared to shoot.

"Okay. Wait," Marc said, stopping her once more. "Your form is terrible! No wonder you are having trouble with this game!"

Dar gave Marc another look of disgust, and stood up again.

"You'll thank me later," he said in response.

*This kid is so arrogant,* Dar thought. Still, she found herself suppressing a smile.

"Let me see how you form your left hand to shoot," Marc commanded.

Dar curved the fingers of her left hand the way she would if she were holding a cue stick. Then, she held it up for Marc to look at.

"Your left hand looks like a claw," he said insultingly. "Let me see how you hold the pool stick."

Dar self-consciously deposited the pool stick between her first and second fingers. She tentatively placed her hand on the table. The position did feel exceedingly awkward. Still, she felt apprehensive about the critique she knew she was about to receive.

"Who taught you to play pool?" Marc asked, staring accusingly at Jeff and Julie.

"Don't look at us," Julie said. "We're not responsible

for that disastrophe."

Marc leaned over and gently adjusted Dar's fingers so that they were in the correct position. "Don't hold it so tightly," he said.

He adjusted her right hand too, so that she wasn't choking up on the pool stick the way she had been. He guided the movements of her arm and wrist so that she could feel how to make the pool stick glide through her fingers.

"Okay, line up the shot," he said.

"I'm afraid if I move, I won't ever get back into this position," she replied.

"Of course you will," he said reassuringly.

"Where am I supposed to hit it, again?" Dar asked.

Marc drew the line with his finger a second time.

"Don't lift the back end of the pool stick so much. Keep it level. Remember, keep your fingers loose on your left hand," he added.

"Okay. Okay. Just let me shoot," Dar said. She had to admit that her hand and her body did feel much more comfortable.

*I'm just gonna shoot this damn thing, and whatever happens, happens,* she thought.

She calmed herself down. She focused her mind. She took a deep breath and said a little prayer. She slid the cue stick back and forth a few times. Then, she pushed the cue stick forward forcefully. There was a *crack* as the cue ball smashed into the target ball which, in the blink of an eye, dropped into the corner pocket, just as Dar had intended. The cue ball, having done its job, came leisurely rolling back towards her.

"Whoa," Marc said. "You almost look like you know what you're doing."

The rest of the room groaned.

"What? You can't be a little happy for her?" Marc asked.

"It's just that now she gets to shoot again, and your whole 'school-of-pool' takes so long," Sean said.

*Oh yeah, now I have to shoot again. Drat!* Dar thought.

"Don't worry, Sean. I think I've got this," Dar said with fake confidence. "Marc, just show me where to shoot."

Marc examined the table.

"Aim the cue ball along this line. It will hit the 4-ball on the outer edge and knock it in."

Dar did as she was told. She lined up the shot. She checked herself to make sure she was forming her left hand correctly and holding the cue stick the way Marc had shown her. She focused. She gave a few practice swipes. Then, she guided the cue stick forward with force. Magically, the cue ball hit the 4-ball just where Marc had said it would and knocked it into their pocket.

Dar stood up. She stared in the direction of the now invisible 4-ball. *Hmmm,* she thought aimlessly.

There was a commotion in the room.

Marc grabbed her by her upper arm and shook her a little. "I can't believe you pocketed that," he said.

"Wow, Dar," Ariel added. "You're doing great! Marc, you're a really good teacher 'cause normally Dar is terrible."

"Thanks, Ariel," Dar responded dryly.

*Now what?* she wondered. *If I make one more shot, I may have to rethink my whole identity as a very bad pool player.*

"You have one more decent shot," Marc said.

"The 5-ball?" she asked.

"Yeah. Hit it right here." He showed her with his finger.

"Okay. I'll give it a shot," she said. "Get it?" She gave Marc a little shove.

"Oh," he groaned. "That was a terrible joke."

Dar leaned over. She placed her cue stick in the proper position. She sighed. Then, she did her best to focus one more time. A second later she stood up. She took another critical look at the alignment of the cue ball and its target. Marc stood looking on, arms crossed, not saying a word.

Dar leaned over again, this time aiming the cue stick at a slightly different angle. She took a few practice swipes and then carefully took the shot. The cue ball hit its target sending the 5-ball towards their pocket. It sailed in easily.

Dar held out her fist to Marc, while the rest of the group erupted in commotion.

"Dar, that was amazing!" Ariel lauded her. "Three in a row. I don't think you've ever even sunk three balls in one game before, let alone three in a row."

"We shouldn't have given her the do-over," Sean said sourly. "We gave her the do-over, and look what's happening – she's winning."

"Maybe you and Marc will beat Julie and Sean," Danni suggested naively.

Dar and Marc looked at each other.

"Uhhh, no!" Dar answered her. "I'm pretty sure we're not going to beat Julie . . . and Sean," she added.

"Yeah," Marc agreed. "We're just happy Dar wasn't a complete fail, right Dar?" He gave her a little shove to match the one she had given him earlier.

*A complete fail?* Dar was indignant. But then, how could she feel insulted when what he said was true? Of course, she was happy she wasn't a "complete fail."

"Yeah, that's right," Dar agreed dully.

*Lighten up!* she thought. *It's only a game of pool, not my reason for living!*

"The next ball is going to be the hardest one for you, Dar," Julie said, turning the group's attention back to the game. "It doesn't look like you have any clear shots."

Dar and Marc retrained their focus on the pool table. There were no target balls even remotely in alignment with their pocket.

*Oh good, the pressure is off,* Dar thought.

"That's okay. I'll just shoot at something random," she offered.

"Dar, let me pick the next shot for you," Julie said. "Here's the shot I would try for." She hopped off her stool and approached the pool table.

"Aim the cue ball right here," she said, pointing to a spot on the side rail. "It will bounce off the rail at this angle." Here, Julie traced the angle with her finger on the green felt.

"If you do it just right, the cue ball will hit the 8-ball, and then, the 8-ball will knock the 3-ball into the pocket. You have to hit the cue ball very precisely on this line to make the correct angle." Julie again traced the line for Dar.

"And, you will have to hit it hard, so that there is enough force to put the whole sequence into motion," she explained.

"Oh my God, are you insane?" Dar asked, looking at her friend incredulously.

Julie smiled.

"Dar, you can make that . . . maybe . . . well? Okay, it's a longshot, but what do you have to lose?" Julie encouraged her.

"Yeah, Dar, go for it," Jeff said. "What do you have to lose?"

"Dar, Dar, Dar," Drew started.

"Dar, Dar, Dar," Ariel, Danni, and Marc added their voices.

"Dar, Dar, Dar," Jeff, Julie, and Sean joined in.

"Dar, Dar, Dar. . ."

"Okay, okay. Shut up," Dar said. "Where am I supposed to aim again?"

"Right here," Julie said as she traced her finger along the path the ball needed to take one more time.

So, for the fourth time that day, Dar leaned over the pool table, pool stick in hand. She kept her eye on the cue ball as well as on the exact spot where Julie had told her to aim. She shaped her hand the way Marc had shown her. She took two practice swipes and went for contact on the third.

The cue ball hit the side rail hard. It bounced off, sailing in the direction of the 8-ball, just as Julie had predicted. It made contact with its target, but instead of hitting the 8-ball squarely in the center, the cue ball just nicked the edge causing the 8-ball to lamely spin off to the side, thus ending Dar's run of successful shots.

"Awwwhhhhh!" groaned the former cheering squad.

"Good effort, good effort," Drew said.

Marc put his hand on Dar's shoulder. "Nice try," he said quietly.

"Okay, who's next?" Jeff queried. "Ariel, you're up."

Ariel jumped up. She approached the pool table

in her inimitable bouncy way. The only blond in the group, Ariel was tall, frothy, and absolutely gorgeous. Gobs of wavy blond hair dangled from her head. She had liquid blue eyes that you could dive into and swim around in. She had a reckless confidence that made you think that she could not be intimidated by anyone or anything.

Ariel picked up the cue stick that Dar had left behind.

"I would have to go after Dar," she said. In reality, she did not care one bit. She chalked the tip of her cue stick while she examined the pool table. She found her shot immediately. She put down the chalk, took aim, and fired with force. The cue ball definitively smacked the target ball. The target ball dropped into her and Drew's pocket.

"Savage," Drew exclaimed.

"You get a lot of practice hanging around with Julie," Ariel explained.

Ariel quickly took her next shot, again pocketing the ball. She waited only a few seconds for the cue ball to come to a halt before leaning in to take her third shot. It, too, landed the target ball in her pocket.

Ariel stood up. "That's it. I'm done," she announced, putting the cue stick down.

"But you have one more turn coming," Drew responded.

"There isn't another shot I can make," Ariel replied.

"You're not going to even try?" Drew asked, baffled by his partner's attitude.

"Nope," Ariel said definitively.

"She does this all the time," Julie interjected, picking up the cue stick that Ariel had left behind.

"I know my limitations," Ariel said, seating herself comfortably on the arm of Drew's chair.

There were eight balls remaining on the table. Julie sank four, temporarily putting her and Sean in the lead. However, Jeff was determined not lose to his sister again. He put away the remaining four balls, and combined with Danni's one, Jeff and Danni won the game with a total of five balls deposited into their pocket.

"Yeah, baby!" Jeff exclaimed as the last ball vanished into his pocket. He carelessly tossed his cue stick aside and thrust both of his arms up into the air, dancing around in victory. Then, he threw his arms around Danni and gave her a big hug. The rest of the group put down their cue sticks and turned their attention to other matters.

"I'm hungry. Does anyone want to order pizza?" Drew asked.

"I do. I'm starving," Marc said.

"I'm in," Jeff agreed as he picked up his discarded pool stick and hung it on the rack.

"Yeah, I can't," Sean said. "I have to get my dad's car back to him."

"My mom's expecting me home," Danni said.

"Mine too," Dar added. She turned away from the group intending to retrieve her phone and collect her things, but Marc unexpectedly grabbed her hand.

"Oh stay," he said to her without letting go. He held onto her hand and gently swung it back and forth just a little. "Text your mom and tell her you're going to stay," he added quietly.

Dar was surprised. Her eyes widened. She stared at Marc, astonished by his pleading.

"I can't," she replied.

"Pleeease," he said, giving her his best puppy face.

Dar took a moment to consider. "No. I really can't. My mother expects me home for dinner," she said at last.

They looked at each other for a long moment. *What's going on here?* Dar wondered, not wanting to look away.

At that instant, Dar became aware that Julie was watching her. She quickly withdrew her hand from Marc's.

"Dar, my mom can give you a ride," Danni said.

"Or Sean can give you a ride," Julie interjected. "Sean goes right by your street. Mrs. Lucci won't have to go out of her way to take you home."

"Where does she live?" Sean addressed this question to Julie, even though Dar was standing right there.

"She lives . . . what's the name of your street, Dar? Laurel Drive? Laurel Drive," Julie said affirmatively. "Sean lives on Red Brook Road, just around the corner from you," she explained to Dar, as if Sean and Dar could only communicate through her.

Dar was silent. She did not want a ride home from Sean. She would definitely prefer to get into a car with good ole Mrs. Lucci and Danni. But Red Brook Road and Laurel Drive were like two minutes from each other, whereas Danni lived clear across town.

It was not that Dar was worried about getting into a car with Sean. She did not fear him or think that he might be a bad driver. She just didn't know him very well. There was both the awkwardness factor and the unpredictability factor. She did not like this plan. She hesitated, hoping that Sean would have a reason why he could not take her.

"Sure, I can take her," Sean said affably, dashing Dar's hopes. "I'm leaving right now, though."

Dar looked helplessly in the direction of Danni, who clearly did not pick up on her discomfort. Besides, asking Mrs. Lucci to drive out of her way when Sean was going right by her street made no sense. She instinctively looked around for Marc, but he had become embroiled in a heated discussion of pizza toppings with Drew and Jeff. So, with no one coming to her rescue, Dar went and got her things.

*It's only a ten-minute drive, fifteen minutes at the most*, she thought. *It's really not a big deal.*

She returned to Sean.

"Ready?" he asked politely.

"Sure," she replied, resigned to her fate.

As they headed towards the sliding glass doors, Dar glanced in the direction of Marc. She wished there could be one more opportunity for a private goodbye. Marc was oblivious, however.

"Dar and Sean are leaving," Julie announced helpfully.

Everyone looked up from what they were doing with a distinct lack of interest. There was a perfunctory chorus of mumbled goodbyes roughly thrown in the direction of Dar and Sean. Sean had already exited, but Dar wheeled around on her heels to look back at her friends.

"Bye," she called out lightly.

She caught Marc's eye momentarily. They looked at each other with a mixture of both longing and uncertainty. And then she was out the door.

△△△

Sean was already in the car with the engine revving when Dar opened the door. She climbed into the front seat beside him. As soon as she closed the door, Sean put the car in reverse and began backing out of the driveway. Dar fumbled with her seatbelt while they were entering the street, but by the time the vehicle was moving forward, she was all strapped in.

"'Sorry for having to take off so quickly," Sean apologized, glancing in her direction while she was trying to figure out the seatbelt. "My dad needs the car before 6:30."

"It's fine," Dar replied. She was surprised that Sean was considering her feelings at all, let alone offering her an apology.

Sean reached out his hand and turned on the car radio. Then he withdrew it and placed it back on the steering wheel.

"Your assignment is to keep us in decent music," he said. "Feel free to press all the buttons and turn as many dials as you like."

"I'm on it," she said.

Dar quickly studied the layout of the controls for the radio in Sean's car: loud/soft dial, search buttons, preset buttons, and the manual search dial. She decided on a course of action, and hit the search button until it landed on her favorite radio station, not that any of the local stations were great, but some were definitely better than others. Fortunately for Dar, the station she wanted was playing a good tune. She turned the volume up, and settled back into her seat.

"Oooooh, slap," Sean said, agreeing with her

choice. He began singing along in a high, light falsetto voice, not exactly on pitch. He stopped, interrupting his own performance.

"Aren't you going to sing with me, Dar?" he asked.

Dar laughed. "No," she said.

"No?" Sean repeated.

"I don't sing in public, " Dar said.

"Not even in the car?" Sean asked. "Everyone sings in the car."

He returned to his falsetto caterwauling. When she did not join him, he stopped again.

"C'mon. It's fun. Are you a bad singer? How bad can you be?"

*Bad,* she thought.

"I'm pretty bad," she said.

"That doesn't stop me," Sean said, and he preceded to demonstrate.

Dar laughed, unsure what to do. She considered her two options: would she feel more embarrassed singing with Sean or not singing with him?

*Oh, what the hell . . .* she decided.

She began singing very, very quietly. After three or four lines, Sean stopped.

"You're right. You are bad," he said.

Dar laughed.

They continued their sing-along until Sean turned

the car onto her street.

"Which house is it?" he asked between snippets of song.

"It's the third one on the right," she replied.

Dar unbuckled her seatbelt. She placed her hand on the door handle, ready to make an exit as soon as the car stopped. The moment the vehicle came to a complete halt, Dar was out the door.

"Thanks," she said as she closed the car door behind her.

"Not a problem," Sean replied. He backed out of the driveway and was gone almost before she could get into the house.

$$\triangle\triangle\triangle$$

It was a little after 6:00 p.m. when Dar entered her house. Dinner was not quite ready, so she headed to her room. She pulled out a small notebook from her backpack and looked over her list of homework assignments. It looked like about an hour's worth of work, maybe a little more; nothing too terrible. She would get started after dinner.

An hour and a half later, Dar was back in her room staring at an algebraic equation. She had only completed three problems and already she was in need of a distraction. She shuffled through her phone looking for her current favorite tune. She hit "Play," then tried to refocus on her work.

Every few minutes, scenes from earlier in the day drifted through her mind, all of them involving Marc. She had had so much fun with him. He was so warm and sweet. He had been so personal with her, so surprisingly intimate. She really wanted to see him again.

*Is he like that with every girl?* she wondered. *Could he seriously be interested in me, or was he just having fun?*

Dar finished two more algebra problems. She decided to text Julie.

"What r u up to?" she asked.

"Watching bb, u?" Julie texted back.

"Alg hw," Dar answered.

"Marc likes u," Julie texted.

Dar felt herself suck in her breath as she read these words. Julie hadn't wasted any time in getting to the point of the communication.

"He asked about u after u left," she continued.

"R u serious?" Dar texted back. Her excitement was growing.

"Come over tomorrow. M will b here."

"Sure," Dar answered.

The texting abruptly ended there. Dar went back

to work on her homework with renewed focus. She tried not to think about Marc anymore. Still, she couldn't help but smile to herself as she worked.

# TUESDAY
## CHAPTER 3

Dar awoke on Tuesday morning still smiling, although at first, she did not remember why. Then, it came to her all at once in a flood of images and feelings - Marc. She pictured him: his silky brown hair, his warm brown eyes, his smile. She thought about each interaction they had had, each snippet of conversation. She reviewed every word he had said to her, wondering if it all added up to anything meaningful? Was he just having fun, or was he was truly interested in her? He did not want her to leave, so that was a good sign. She remembered the lingering touch of his hand. She was definitely into him.

Dar rolled over in her warm bed. She pulled the covers close around her. She savored the moment. She barely knew Marc, and yet, she felt more drawn to him than any other boy she had ever met. She wished she knew for sure how he felt about her.

Moments later her alarm went off, putting an end to her reverie. Dar got out of bed. She practically sprinted to the bathroom to get ready for school. She couldn't stop thinking about Marc, though, even as she went about her morning routine. It suddenly dawned on her that she did not know a thing about him. She had assumed he was a senior at DHS just because he was friends with Julie's brother, Jeff, but she didn't know for sure.

*Why haven't I ever seen him around school before?* she wondered. Perhaps she had seen him at school without realizing it. Maybe she would run into him today. *If only*, she thought.

Dar carefully picked out her clothes for the day: her favorite shredded jeans and a short, white tank with a chunky sweater. The jeans showed off her long legs, while the beige in the sweater brought out the green in her eyes and the reddish hues in her auburn hair.

She was just finishing applying her make-up when her dad yelled up to her. "Dar, if you want a ride, I'm leaving in fifteen minutes."

"Okay," she yelled back.

Dar grabbed her books and headed downstairs. She had just enough time to make herself a cup of hot cocoa and wolf down a granola bar. Her mom came into the kitchen while she was eating.

"Oh, don't you look cute," she said.

"Thanks," Dar replied. After a moment of chewing,

she added, "I'm going to Julie's house after school. I'll text you later if I need a ride."

"Okay," her mother said. "Try to let me know early, before I start dinner."

"Ready?" her dad asked.

Dar picked up her backpack. She checked to make sure she had her cell phone. She followed her father out the front door.

It was a beautiful, sunny day midway through October. The air was unusually mild with just a hint of crispness. It made Dar want to take a deep breath the moment she stepped out the door. A light gust of wind delicately stirred the leaves on the ground. The wind also made a lovely rustling sound in the trees above her.

Dar opened the passenger-side door of the car. She climbed in next to her father. It was going to be a great day.

△△△

Dar was really looking forward to seeing Julie during their first period history class. She had so many questions about Marc. She wanted to know what grade he was in. Did he even go to DHS? What was his last name? Where did he live? She knew absolutely nothing about him.

Dar entered her history class early. She took her

seat. She pulled out her history textbook, a notebook, and a pen. She began to doodle mindlessly as she waited for Julie to arrive, keeping one eye on the clock. As the minutes ticked by, Dar began to feel more and more agitated. If Julie did not arrive soon, they would not have much time to talk. She decided she had better send Julie a text. She pulled her phone out of her bag.

*Damn! I should have checked with her earlier,* Dar thought as she typed.

"Where r u?" she asked.

Moments later, a reply appeared.

"Just woke up," Julie wrote.

"Sloth," Dar wrote back, annoyed.

"I'm baby. Take notes for me," Julie replied.

Dar sighed disappointedly. She put the phone away. She picked up her pen and began doodling again. *Typical Julie,* she thought. The information Dar wanted would have to wait.

First period history class passed by slowly. Dar succeeded in forcing herself to pay attention throughout most of the class, but without Julie, she was bored. Not that she and Julie were rude or disruptive when they were in class together, but Julie was just enough of a distraction to break up the monotony of the lecture. It just took a smile, a look, or a minute doodle for them to create a private joke and entertain themselves. They communicated that well with each other.

Finally, the bell rang. History class was over. Dar picked up her things and headed towards her English class.

*I won't be seeing Julie until lunch now,* she thought. *And there will be too many people around to have a private conversation with her there. I will have to find a way to talk to her during p.e.*

As she walked down the hall thinking about when she could talk to Julie next, Brenda Beckett, a girl Dar knew from the volleyball team, came racing towards her. As Brenda passed by, she swooped in close to Dar's ear and said softly, "Goals! Big jells!"

Dar abruptly stopped walking. She turned her head in the direction of the girl. "Huh?" she mumbled, barely registering the comment, but Brenda was already gone.

*That was weird!* Dar thought.

She reached her English class and entered. She took her seat, still thinking about when she would be able to talk to Julie next.

Moments later, two other sophomore girls, Riley Springer and Lindsay Harris, arrived. They took their seats next to Dar's. No sooner had they sat down when Lindsay turned to Dar.

"Hey," Lindsay said.

"Hey," Dar replied, barely looking up. She had started doodling again. She seemed to be obsessed with doodling today. The excitement over meeting Marc was turning into anxiety, and with no other outlet available to her, Dar found herself channeling her nervous energy into cartoon characters, bouquets of flowers, and small geometric shapes. It was a calming activity, and it seemed to give her comfort.

"So, Dar, what did you do last night?" Lindsay asked with a stealthy glance towards Riley.

Dar stopped doodling and looked up. "Nothing. Just a night in with homework," she said flatly. She stopped doodling, but she did not put down her pen. She was now wiggling it between her fingers as if it were a special effect in a light show.

"What did you do?" Dar perfunctorily reciprocated the question. The conversation was a welcome distraction.

"We heard something else," Riley reported, completely ignoring Dar's question.

"What did you hear?" Dar asked with a distinct lack of interest. She truly had no idea what Riley was talking about, and basically thought the girl had all the social graces of a slug.

"We heard you were *with* someone last night. Who's the guy you're seeing?"

Dar swiveled her eyes in Riley's direction. She knew ten-year-olds with better personalities than these two had. What stupid interaction were they attempting to engage her in now?

"I have no idea what you're talking about," Dar said with revulsion.

*Why do I even concede to speaking to these two?* she wondered contemptuously. *They are so consistently annoying - like a pair of flies constantly buzzing around a mound of poop.*

"The guy you're seeing," Lindsay repeated as if Dar had not understood the first time.

"What guy?" Dar asked. "I'm not 'seeing' any guy."

"Sexting, then?" Lindsay asked tauntingly. Riley laughed.

"No!" Dar replied.

It suddenly dawned on her that they could be talking about Marc. But that would be impossible. For one thing, she wasn't *seeing* Marc.

Dar's mind involuntarily began to run through yesterday's events. There was no possible way these two girls could know about her feelings for Marc. She hadn't talked to anyone about him, not even to Julie, not really.

"The guy you were *with* yesterday?" Riley continued.

"Are you talking about the kid I played pool with yesterday?" Dar asked naively. She was truly confused. Her question was a mistake, however. It was all the ammunition Lindsay and Riley needed to attack her.

"Pool, yes, pool. Was it hot?" Riley asked. She was so obnoxious. Lindsay giggled.

"What are you talking about?" Dar asked snottily. She did not like the tone or the implication of Riley's question.

"Oh, c'mon Dar. Spill the tea. We know you hooked up with a senior last night. Who was it?"

"What? Who told you that?" Dar asked emphatically. She felt herself flush. "I didn't hook up with anybody last night," she replied coolly.

But Lindsay and Riley would not let it go.

"No cap, Dar. It's all over the school. What's his name? Sean something?"

*Sean?* Dar was taken aback. Her brain worked rapidly to try to make sense of what Lindsay and Riley were saying. *Why do they think I hooked up with Sean?* she wondered.

"Sean? Sean?" Dar sneered at them. Daggers of disgust shot from her eyes. "I got a ride home from Julie's friend, Sean. I didn't hook up with him," she said defensively.

*Why am I even explaining myself to these two lemmings?* she wondered. Her demeanor was as cold as ice, but that did not stop Lindsay and Riley.

"Yeah. That's exactly what we heard. Sean gave you a ride. Or, more like, you gave him a ride - down Route 53X," Lindsay said.

Riley laughed. The girls looked at each other in solidarity and smiled cruelly. They were enjoying this game at Dar's expense.

Dar so wanted to tell these two girls to go f-themselves. Instead, she turned away and faced the front of the room. It was her way of letting Lindsay and Riley know that she was done with them. Fortunately, her timing coincided perfectly with Mrs. Collins insisting that the class quiet down, thus preventing further conversation. Dar was seething, though.

*Where do these two girls get off toying with me like that? And where did they get this cringey idea that Sean and I hooked up?*

She tried to calm down and focus on what Mrs. Collins was saying, but it was difficult. The fifty-minute class passed by with agonizing slowness. Finally, the bell rang. Lindsay and Riley took off without saying anything more to her.

Dar grabbed her things. She walked quickly on to her chemistry class. No one else said anything to her along the way; nothing but a few greetings here and there. She began to calm down. Maybe this was nothing.

She entered the chemistry classroom and found Danni there, already in her seat. Very few of her close friends were in her classes. Julie was in her history class. Danni was in her chemistry class. They all had p.e. together, and they all ate lunch together along with Brit Lawson who blended into their group beautifully. Not one of her close friends was in her math, Spanish, or English classes, however.

Dar headed straight for Danni. She unconsciously craved the comforting companionship of a good friend. It had certainly been an unsettling morning. Danni seemed glad to see her.

"Hey," Danni greeted her.

"Hey," Dar replied.

Danni watched Dar take her seat.

"After you left yesterday, that kid Marc was asking all about you," Danni began. "He tried to be all low key about it, but it's pretty clear that he's into you."

Dar's heart pounded. Her interactions with Lindsay and Riley last period had flustered her so much that she had nearly forgotten about Marc. Now she felt her face flush.

"Really?" she asked. "He's so sweet. It would be amazing to go out with him."

"Right? You looked like you were really into him yesterday. That's why . . . I don't understand why you hooked up with Sean last night?" Danni asked quizzically.

*Hooked up with Sean?* The words hit Dar like a slap in the face.

"What? Why would you think that? God no! Why is everyone saying that? He just gave me a ride home!" Dar was emphatic, but Danni looked skeptical.

"How could you not believe me?" Dar asked, reading Danni's facial expression. "Think about it. Sean was completely into Julie yesterday. I was completely into Marc. Why would Sean and I hook up?"

Danni paused. She looked reflective. This train of logic seemed to make sense to her.

"Well," she said slowly, "I did think it was weird. But then, Sean is kind of cute with his spikey, yellow hair and gray-blue eyes. And you did leave with him."

"I did not leave *with* him," Dar said emphatically. "He took me home. I mean, he drove me home as in . . . dropped me off in my driveway and left. He left, and I went into the house - alone! He did not come in. We did not go anywhere else. . ."

Dar kept adding clarifying statements to her initial assertion. No matter how hard she tried to explain what had happened, no matter how she described it, there still seemed to be room for misinterpretation and innuendo. Finally, she gave up.

"Okay, okay, I believe you. Calm down," Danni reassured her.

Dar slumped in her seat. If it took this much effort to convince Danni, her close friend, that she had not hooked up with Sean, then what hope did she have of convincing the rest of the school?

Dar stared straight ahead and was silent. She tried to wrap her mind around what was happening in her life. She wanted to ask Danni the question that was really bugging her, but she hesitated. She was afraid to hear the answer. Finally, her need to know overrode her apprehension.

"Who. . . how. . .?" Dar started. She sputtered. "Who is spreading this rumor about me and Sean?"

she finally managed to spit out.

"Uhhhh, that's hard to say," Danni responded. "Wendy Walker told me about the rumor. She got a text from somebody. She asked me about you and Sean at the end of last period. Dar, you're going to kill me, but . . . I told her it was true."

Dar received this information as if she had been kicked in the stomach. It took a moment for her to process all the implications of what Danni was saying. Wendy Walker was a girl that Dar barely knew. Why was she receiving texts about Dar at all? This meant that kids Dar didn't even know were texting about her. And Danni had stupidly confirmed the rumor. Dar was mortified.

*How can Danni be so brainless? How could she not come to my defense?* Dar was livid.

Dar was aware of various rumors that had circulated around the school in the past: Ayden Bryce only got the lead in the school play because his parents complained; Kaley London made out with her best friend's boyfriend, and that's why they were no longer friends; Russel Chang cheated on Mariah Welch with Alena Marques while Mariah was recovering from COVID; Logan Brown and Gary Patrelli were caught drinking in the boys' locker room, but the p.e. teacher covered it up so that they could continue to play football. The list went on.

Dar did not know for sure if all these rumors were true, but she had no reason to doubt them.

They were regarded as truth among the student body. The rumors were circulated by friends of the alleged victims or kids who claimed to have witnessed the acts. Some of these rumors formed the basis for conflicts among groups of students. Often, they erupted into warring exchanges on social media. It never occurred to Dar that any one of them might be purely made up.

Dar, Julie, and their friends did not troll their classmates. They did not engage in creating malicious posts about other kids. They did enjoy the role of audience whenever a good drama erupted, however. Most of what they read was purely vindictive, but that did not stop them from sharing it and talking about it with each other. What could it hurt after all? They made up their own names and their own language for discussing the kids in their school - at least the ones that were worth discussing.

Of course, none of Dar's friends would be directly mean or nasty to anyone. Occasionally, however, Julie and Ariel did take their games too far. Like the time when there were no empty tables in the cafeteria, so they all had to sit with this painfully shy girl named - of all things - "Clarissa." Julie and Ariel discussed the poor girl the entire time by pretending that they were talking about Ariel's dog, Rassie. In actuality, they were talking about Clarissa. It was funny in a vicious sort of way. It made Dar uncomfortable, but at the same time, Julie and Ariel were so clever in the way they disguised their conversation that it was all Dar could do to keep from laughing.

Then, one of the girls focused on a hideous piece of clothing that Clarissa was wearing and began complimenting her on it. They all joined in. After Clarissa left the table, they waited just long enough for her to be out of earshot before they all burst out laughing.

They continued their game for the next few days, discussing anyone they wanted by calling the person "Rassie." Eventually, Ariel decided that her dog was too cute and too sweet to allow his name to be misused in that way.

Generally, though, they were not that nasty. They were just selective about who they chose to hang with.

Periodically, Julie would connect with someone from outside their friend-group, an upperclassman usually. Julie would invite her and her whole squad to a girls' night-in at Julie's house. Those parties were really fun, and Dar got to know a lot of the juniors and seniors that way. Sometimes, too, Julie's brother Jeff would host parties for the senior class. Julie, Dar, Ariel, and Danni would always be included.

These connections made Dar recognizable around the school. Now she was paying the price. If some no-life girl had gotten a ride home from Sean, nobody would have even cared - except maybe to talk about Sean.

△△△

The bell rang. Chemistry was over. Dar stood up heavily. She gathered her things. She wondered what was in store for her on the way to her next class. Danni breezily said "goodbye" and floated out the classroom door, completely oblivious to Dar and her problems.

Dar was on her own. She headed to her locker to switch books before Spanish class. She narrowed her eyes and stared straight ahead as she walked. She tried to look as cold and as disdainful as possible so that no one would talk to her. She wore the haughty mask of superiority, pretending not to see anyone. She made herself completely unapproachable. It was a way for her to dominate, to control the situation, a way for her to send the message to everyone she encountered not to mess with her. She was the unapproachable ice queen. If she could not control what kids were saying about her behind her back, at least she could control what they were saying to her face. And maybe her attitude, her projection of power, would intimidate everyone into not talking about her at all. She hardened her eyes so that no warmth and no light emitted from them - only ice-cold arrogance and hatred.

The walk to Spanish turned out to be uneventful. The mask worked. It protected Dar in the moment. It gave her a sense of control over the situation. But it did not make her feel any less vulnerable deep inside.

Dar entered her Spanish class with her new facade intact. It was the look of a snotty, dismissive girl, as if everyone around her had no importance in her life. No one was worthy of her time or attention. She had seen Julie wear this mask a thousand times before, and while it did not come as easily to Dar as it did to Julie, she still knew just how to produce it for maximum affect; how to manipulate and control through narrowing her eyes; how to dominate through sneering and ignoring. She was one of the *G Girls* after all. No one would dare speak disrespectfully to her without suffering a consequence.

Spanish II was one of those classes that had a blend of different grades. The majority of the students in the class were frosh who had studied Spanish throughout middle school. The second largest group were sophomores who had begun taking Spanish in high school. There was a small group of juniors who had failed the class the first time around. And, there was one senior who was planning on majoring in foreign languages in college.

Dar was not worried about the frosh in the class. *Would they have heard the rumor about me and Sean?* She thought it was unlikely. And even if they had, it would probably make her seem even more beyond them.

Dar was not worried about the juniors because they were mostly boys who had flunked Spanish II the first time around - not the highest wattage bulbs in the pack, and certainly not kids that Dar cared about.

The sophomores were worrisome, however. They were the group most likely to have spread the rumor about her because they all knew her. She and Julie had set themselves apart from the rest of the sophomore class, so they were also the group most likely to want to take her down a notch.

And then there was the one senior in the class, Elyse Serano. Dar sat next to Elyse. And Dar did care about what Elyse thought of her.

Dar had met Elyse at one of Julie's "girls only" parties, and although their acquaintance had been neither long nor deep, they found each other on the first day of Spanish II class and sat together out of necessity, since neither one of them had a close friend in the class.

Dar liked Elyse. She was intelligent, dope, and very self-assured. She stood out among the rest of the kids in the class as a mature girl who had her act together. Elyse was planning on majoring in foreign languages. She was already in her sixth year of French and had added Spanish in her junior year.

Elyse was currently in the process of applying to colleges. She frequently talked with their teacher, Mrs. Delgado, before class. They usually discussed the colleges Elyse had visited over the weekend, which colleges she should apply to, and how stressful the whole process was. Because Dar sat next to Elyse, she was also included in these discussions, although she did not have much to contribute. Naturally, Elyse was Mrs. Delgado's favorite student in the class, and because Mrs. Delgado perceived Dar to be Elyse's friend, Dar was also given "favorite" status.

Dar entered Spanish early. She was not about to stand around in the hallway socializing - not today. She glided past the few frosh that were already in the classroom. Elyse had not yet arrived. Dar took her seat in the front row, determined not to turn around - ever.

As she sat there waiting, Dar's icy attitude faded into worry.

*What if Elyse heard the rumor about me and Sean?* she wondered. *What will she think of me then?*

Elyse would be very familiar with everyone in the senior class. She most likely knew Sean. She could very well know Marc, too. And, just as the rumor was circulating around the sophomore class, it was probably also circulating around the senior class.

Dar wondered what Elyse thought of Sean. Would she believe a rumor about the two of them? And what if one of the vindictive sophomores said something to purposely embarrass Dar in front of Elyse? How would she handle that?

Dar set her jaw defensively and waited. She prayed that Mrs. Delgado would start the class before anyone had a chance to humiliate her.

As the minutes ticked by, Dar's thoughts drifted to Marc. She wondered if Elyse knew Marc. She wanted to ask Elyse if Marc was in the senior class, but she didn't even know his last name. What would she say?

*Do you know a kid named 'Marc'? Or maybe, Is*

there a kid named 'Marc' in the senior class?

Even under the best of circumstances, those questions sounded idiotic. How would Dar explain them?

*I met him yesterday, and I'm in love with him. I'm just trying to figure out who he is.*

*Like reverse gender Cinderella*, Dar mused. *Cinderello and I'm the princess. If only I had his shoe.*

She smiled to herself and continued her imaginary conversation with Elyse. *Oh, and by the way, I only got a ride home from Sean Parker. I did not 'go home,' 'go for a ride,' 'hook up,' 'make out,' or 'do the nasty,' with him."*

It all sounded sus. She might as well just send out her own text validating any and all rumors about herself.

Elyse entered the classroom just as the bell was ringing. She quietly sat down next to Dar. As if in answer to Dar's prayers, Mrs. Delgado started the class the second Elyse was in her seat. There was no opportunity for them to speak.

As the class got underway, Dar snuck a furtive glance in Elyse's direction. Elyse did not seem like her usual self. She definitely seemed cold and distant. Dar began to worry.

*Damn! She must have heard the rumor*, Dar thought.

It was an uncomfortable fifty minutes. Dar sat

hunched over in a self-protective stance. She felt sheepish even though she had done nothing wrong. Elyse dutifully concentrated on the class. When the bell rang, Elyse hopped up to talk privately with Mrs. Delgado, shutting Dar out altogether.

Despite her concerns about Elyse, Dar felt relief more than anything else now that Spanish was over. She left the classroom in a hurry. She proceeded to the cafeteria, briefly stopping by her locker to drop off her books. She was looking forward to being with her friends at lunch. She needed to feel the sense of safety and protection that they afforded her.

As Dar entered the cafeteria, she felt her cheeks involuntarily flush and turn red. She hadn't expected that. She suddenly felt self-conscious. She knew that kids had been talking about her all morning. She wasn't sure who. She wondered if people were staring at her. She couldn't tell.

She tried not to look at anyone directly as she briskly walked to the table where Julie, Ariel, and Danni were sitting along with their friend Brit Lawson. However, if Dar thought she was going to get some relief by being with her friends, she was woefully mistaken. As soon as she caught sight of Julie's smirking face, she knew she was in for it. They were going to tease her mercilessly.

"Dar, you little thot," Julie began. "I hear you've been getting busy!"

"First Marc, then Sean," Ariel piled on. "Do you

have someone else lined up for later today, Dar?"

"The Ferret," Julie said grinning, referring to Robert Ferrier who had been Dar's dance partner on the night of the fight.

"You guys just suck! This is a horror show," Dar responded. "And Danni didn't help anything by telling Wendy Walker that it was true."

Julie and Ariel started laughing. Brit looked confused.

"Well, I didn't know," Danni said sheepishly.

"You couldn't figure it out?" Dar replied, practically yelling at her.

"Wait," Brit entered the conversation. "What really happened, Dar? Did you go home with this guy or not?"

"No, I did not go home with him! Absolutely not. He's one of Julie's friends. He just gave me a ride home." Dar stated her case one more time.

"How do we know he brought you directly home?" Julie asked, further needling her. "You could have easily taken the long route by the cliffs."

"I assure you, we did not go by the cliffs," Dar said snottily. "I left your house at 5:45, and I was home by 6:00." She was quickly tiring of this game.

"Do you know who started the rumor, Dar?" Brit asked sympathetically. She was so sweet. She was genuinely concerned for Dar.

"No, I don't," Dar replied in a deflated tone. She

looked at each one of her friends, and for the first time, it occurred to her that it could have been one of them.

"It was probably one of the guys," Ariel said.

"Guys are more gossipy than girls," Danni asserted.

"It was probably Sean," Julie said. "'Probably just a flex for his friends. Dar, you would definitely be an upgrade for him."

Ariel interrupted the conversation. "Nate Cassidy just sent me this," she said. "He doesn't say where he got it from, though."

Ariel held out her phone so that Dar, Brit, Danni, and Julie could read it. It was a copy of a text exchange. It said:

- *Sean scored a gorgy last night*

- *Which one?*

- *Dar*

- *I thought he was stan Julie*

- *Does it matter? Dar's the hottest anyway*

- *Disagree*

"Oh my God, Dar! That's awful!" Danni exclaimed.

"Wait, are you talking about Sean Parker?" Brit asked.

The girls nodded.

"'You know him?" Julie asked.

"Yes, I know him. Skeazy," Brit replied. "I bet he

started the rumor himself."

*Freakin' Sean*, Dar thought. *I can't believe he did this to me!*

△△△

The school day seemed to go on forever. Lunch was followed by p.e. The conversation among the girls in Dar's p.e. class as they were changing their clothes in the girls' locker room went like this:

- Dar, how did you get Sean to take you home? I only ever see him with Julie. How did you get him to be with you?

- That's true, Dar. What did you do? You don't seem like you can compete with Julie. Is she mad at you now?

- Guys, why would Julie be mad? If she really had wanted to be with Sean, she could have been. If Dar wants to be with Sean, then why should Sean deny her?

- It makes sense. Sean couldn't be with Julie, so he got with Dar.

- You make her sound like a Julie sub.

- Well, yeah.

After the class moved onto the playing field, the talk became bolder and more crass.

- Kick it to Dar, she's an expert at handling balls.

- She got a good work-out yesterday.

- Just ask Sean about her mad skills.

- Dar, how *long* was the ride?

- Dar, you know we love you.

The dual conditions of locker room mentality and competitive activity seemed to give every sophomore girl in Dar's p.e. class permission to say whatever they wanted to her. Her classmates banded together like a pack of wolves on the hunt, laughing at each other's jokes and encouraging further aggression. Pent-up anger and hostilities came flying out. As long as her classmates were together and making jokes for each other, they saw nothing wrong with using her as the target.

Dar so wanted to clap back, but the situation was too overwhelming. Denial wasn't going to work, and she wasn't skilled at exchanging verbal attacks. Julie and Ariel were no help. They thought the whole thing was a big joke and seemed to be enjoying her misery.

In the end, the entire experience actually reinforced her attitude of superiority over her classmates.

*These stupid comments are why I don't hang around with these immature insects in the first place,* she thought.

△△△

Her last period of the day was math. Exhausted, Dar sank into her seat next to Robert Ferrier. Robert was just about to speak when Dar's phone pinged. She pulled it out. There was a text from Julie.

*I just left her,* Dar thought. *What does she want now?*

The text was sent to all the *G Girls*. It read, "My mom has a migraine. No friends."

*Probably just as well,* Dar thought. She was exhausted; she had a ton of homework; she didn't exactly feel like being with her friends; and most significantly, she did not think she could face Marc.

*Did he hear the rumor?* she wondered. *What does he think of me now?* She really didn't want to know the answers to those questions.

Robert started to speak again, but Dar held up one finger signaling for him to hold off. She quickly typed out a text asking her mother to pick her up from school at 2:35 p.m. Dar had barely hit "send" when Mr. Reed began to speak, signaling the start of class.

Dar scrambled to take out her math book, paper, and a pencil. She shut off the sound on her phone and then slowly lowered it into her book bag, watching the screen as it went. She hoped that her mother would respond before the phone disappeared entirely.

She was just about to release it into the bag when a small "k" appeared on the screen. Dar felt her shoulders relax. Fortunately, her mother had received the message and had responded quickly.

Dar tucked the phone away in her bag. She settled herself into her chair. She turned her attention towards Mr. Reed. She was relieved that this was the last class of the day. Knowing that she was going home directly afterwards made her feel almost normal. P.E. had been physically and emotionally draining. She had no more energy with which to fret or worry. She just had to get through this one class, and then she could go home.

Finally, the bell rang. Again, Robert attempted to say something, but Dar stopped him. "Not you too," she said. "He just gave me a ride. Nothing happened."

"I never thought anything did," Robert replied. "I figured it was just a stupid rumor. All I was going to say was, you must be having a really bad day."

Without a moment's hesitation, Dar gave Robert a kiss on the cheek and a big hug. She could have cried for his kindness.

ΔΔΔ

At 2:35 p.m., Dar was on the sidewalk in front of Deerfield High School, waiting for her mother to pick her up. Her locker was close to the main entrance of the school, close enough anyway, so that she was able to get out of the building quickly. Now, she stood waiting patiently on the sidewalk alongside kids she did not know, kids who were also waiting for their rides.

All around her was commotion. Cars and busses were crammed together, vying with each other for a piece of the curb. Kids streamed past her on both sides, running for their rides, or trying to catch up with their friends. The air was filled with general crowd noises: chatter, exuberant laughter, and joyous screams. The explosive release of pent-up energy that had been previously suppressed in classrooms was palpable. Occasionally, someone she knew ran past her, acknowledging her presence with a "hey."

"Hey," she replied back. No one stopped to tease or question her. They were all just glad to be free from school.

Dar had been standing there less than two minutes when she saw her mother swing the car up to the curb. Thankfully, her mother was on time.

Dar opened the passenger side door. She plopped down into the front seat, backpack and all. She would have put her stuff in the backseat except for the fact that her two, younger sisters, Maria and Carly, were back there. Apparently, Maria, age 10, had been aggravating Carly, age 8. Mrs. Blaise was speaking sternly to the two of them when Dar opened the car door. She waited for Dar to get in before explaining.

"Your sisters had a half-day today," she said. "They have been driving me crazy all afternoon. They won't stop picking on each other. I need to get them outside."

As an after thought she added, "How was your day?"

"It was fine," Dar replied.

She tried to sound as light hearted as possible in her response. She really did not want to discuss the details of her day with her mother. Fortunately, Mrs. Blaise's attention was quickly drawn away from Dar by the dual demands of both navigating the traffic and mediating between her two younger daughters. Dar was left free to remain in the privacy of her own thoughts. It had been one nightmare of a day. She was ready to go home.

Once at home, Dar changed into the most comfortable clothing she could find: a soft, warm, comfy hoodie and drawstring pants. She made herself a cup of tea. She looked over her list of homework assignments: math and chemistry problems, reading for history, a paper for English, and some written exercises for Spanish. For once in her life, she was grateful for a lot of homework. She would not have time to think about anything else for the rest of the day. She settled down and got to work.

Around 8:00 p.m., Dar decided to text Julie. She wondered if Marc had come over, and if he had asked about her again. *Although,* she reasoned, *if Julie* couldn't have friends over, then Jeff probably couldn't either.

She wondered if Marc had heard the rumor? Or if Sean and Jeff had discussed it with him?

*Probably,* she answered her own questions. *I guess I can kiss that sweet fairy tale goodbye.*

She texted Julie.

*"What r u up to?"*

There was no reply.

*That's odd,* Dar thought. *Julie is never out of reach of her phone.*

# WEDNESDAY

## CHAPTER 4

Dar tumbled into bed around 9:30 p.m., but she couldn't sleep. Scenes from earlier in the day drifted in and out of her mind. She felt unsettled. She loathed the idea of going back to school in the morning. She tossed and turned, unable to get comfortable. She couldn't stop feeling apprehensive about the following day.

*I could stay home tomorrow,* she plotted. *I could definitely stay home. I can get all my assignments online. I'll be able to do all my homework. I already have my books. I could hand in my English paper through the portal. And I don't have any tests.*

It was a definite possibility. She decided to leave the option open.

Comforted by the fact that she now had a plan and the option of a skip day to save her from further indignations, Dar drifted off to sleep.

ΔΔΔ

She awoke before her alarm went off and lay in bed. In a few minutes, she would have to make a decision about whether to go to school. What excuse could she use? *Sore throat? Nausea? Cramps?*

She decided she would tell her parents that her head hurt and her stomach ached. After yesterday, neither excuse was all that far from the truth.

She continued to lay in bed waiting for the alarm.

*If I stay home today,* she reasoned, *by tomorrow everyone will have forgotten about me and about the rumor, or at least most kids will. It's possible that they have already forgotten.*

She knew this to be true. Once a rumor made the rounds, kids stopped talking about it. Although, in her case, there could be some long-term damage to her image, not only because everyone now had a juicy piece of gossip with which to demean her, but also because they had demonstrated to each other that they had no fear of using it. The reverence for her status as a *G Girl* had been demolished; the illusion of her invulnerability, shattered.

*Oh no,* she thought suddenly. *What if more texts circulate about me and Sean today? I'll have to endure a whole new round of humiliation.*

Dar felt the knot congeal in the pit of her stomach. *Maybe I really don't feel well,* she thought.

Dar rolled over. She pulled the covers up over her head. She groaned. She decided to stop thinking about any of it. She decided to forget about it all. She intentionally banished all thoughts of the rumor, Marc, Sean, school, and everything else from her mind. She took a deep breath and focused on the present moment. She felt her body relax as she greedily sank into the warmth of her bed, into a feeling of peace. And then, just for a few seconds, she drifted back into sleep.

Minutes later her alarm went off. Jolted from her sleep, Dar sprang out of bed. All of a sudden, she was angry, maybe angrier than she had ever been before.

*I am going to school*, she decided. *I'm not going to let my rumor-mongering, cretin classmates intimidate me into staying home. Why should my life be disrupted by a bunch of jerks with nothing better to do than pass texts about me?*

No! She would face the fire.

## △△△

An hour and ten minutes later, Dar was in the car en route to school. Her mother was at the wheel. As they approached Deerfield High, Dar felt the butterflies begin to flutter in her stomach once more. Her moment of bravado had passed, and now she just hoped that she was making the right decision. At least she had the comfort of knowing that Julie would be with her during first period, assuming that Julie was on time today. As annoying as Julie could be, she was still Dar's best friend, and Dar felt stronger when the two of them were together. Besides, she still had so many questions she wanted to ask Julie about Marc.

They pulled up to the main entrance of the school.

"Are you going to need a ride home today?" her mother asked.

"'Not sure yet," Dar replied. "I'll text you."

Dar grabbed her backpack. She took a deep breath and opened the door.

"Bye mom," she called.

"Bye sweetie. Love you."

"Love you, too." She slammed the door behind her.

△△△

Dar arrived in history class a full fifteen minutes early and without incident. She sat down. She took a notebook, a pen, and her phone out of her bag. She was in the process of texting Julie when Julie appeared in the doorway of the classroom carrying a large Java Palooza coffee cup, early for once.

"Hey," Julie said.

"Hey," Dar responded. "I was just texting you."

"Jeff had to get to school early this morning, so I made him take me to Java Palooza first," Julie explained without Dar asking.

Dar couldn't help noticing that, even first thing in the morning, Julie was electric. Even half-awake, she still entered the classroom in a whirlwind of energy. She was tall and stunning with long black hair, surprisingly deep blue eyes, defined cheek bones, and pinky-white skin. She had the lean and strong body of an athlete, and she made no apologies for it. This morning, she had on a pair of leggings with high-tops. Her powdery blue sweater draped softly over her shoulders and revealed a pierced navel, making her look bold and daring. Some silver and stone jewelry adorned her neck and lightly complemented her clothing. But it was not her striking image, nor her sense of personal style that commanded attention. No, it was a projection of authority and a mild disregard for others because, unlike most of her classmates, Juliette Lyons was absolutely sure of herself.

Julie dropped a small, vegan-leather backpack onto her desk. She seated herself next to it. She put the toes of her sneakers on the edge of her chair for balance. She cradled her massive cup of coffee with both hands and stared down at Dar.

"What did you end up doing last night?" Dar asked her with curiosity. "I texted you but you never texted me back."

"Oh . . . yeah," Julie replied, taking a sip of her coffee. "I didn't get your text until around 11:00 p.m. I went to the movies. I had to get out of the house. I was so bored."

"By yourself? What did you go see?" Dar asked.

"I saw *Dark Matter*?" Julie answered, taking another sip.

"Never heard of it," Dar said.

"It's a sci-fi thriller. Mostly takes place on a spaceship," Julie offered.

"Is that the movie with Ty Adams and Quinten Baker-Phillips?" Dar asked.

"Uh-huh. That's the one," Julie answered.

"Was it good? What was it about?" Dar asked.

"They go on a mission to investigate dark matter, and - "

"Wait. What's 'dark matter'?" Dar interrupted.

"I don't know. They never really explained it."

"Well, is it a real thing, or is it something made up for the movie?"

"I don't know, Dar. It was a sci-fi thriller, not a PBS special."

"But the movie is called *Dark Matter*," Dar said. "They must have said something about it."

"It's some kind of matter that they think is part of the universe, but they don't really know if it exists. The premise of the movie is that they are on a mission to find it and prove its existence. Happy?" Julie asked, exasperated.

"Yes. Thank you. Was that so hard? I thought you hated sci-fi movies."

"I do, but this was more of an action slash suspense slash thriller slash horror film."

"Seriously?" Dar responded.

"Yes, Dar, seriously," Julie continued. "They think they've found the dark matter, but it turns out that what they actually found was an alien species. Just as the dark matter threatens to absorb them, they are rescued by another alien species, only to be enslaved by them. The rest of the movie is about their escape."

"That sounds really bad," Dar said.

"It sounds really bad, but actually, it was pretty good. A lot of action, some good special effects, and Quinten Baker-Philips is TDF.

"Who did you go with? Jeff?" Dar asked.

"Um, well, no," Julie hesitated slightly. "Jeff went to Drew's. But Marc stopped by. He was looking for Jeff, and since Jeff wasn't home, I asked him if he wanted to go to the movies," she said casually.

*Marc?* Dar was completely caught off guard.

"Who Marc? You mean the Marc we played pool with on Monday? My Marc?"

Dar realized the absurdity of what she was saying, even as the words were coming out of her mouth. Marc did not belong to her. They had only met each other once. She did not even know his last name. They hadn't even gone out on one date. She did not know for sure if he really liked her. Marc was a very long way from being hers. Still, she felt that Julie had somehow

93

crossed a line.

"Yeah," Julie said carelessly. "Jeff wasn't home. Neither of us had anything to do. I couldn't invite him in because of my mother. So, I asked him if he wanted to go to the movies. That's all we did."

*That's all? That's all?* Dar was completely outraged. *Is Julie that clueless?* She wondered.

"Julie, you know how I feel about him!" Dar hissed.

"What? It was nothing," Julie stated emphatically. "We just went to the movies as friends. It didn't mean anything. Besides, you and I never got a chance to talk yesterday. How was I supposed to know how you felt about him?"

Dar closed her mouth hard. What could she say? It was true that Julie had not actually violated any friend code. Marc was not Dar's boyfriend. She had no real premise for accusing Julie of anything. Still, she felt very, very angry. Somewhere in the ambiguity of her emotions, Dar felt she was being undermined.

"You're not going to get all reactive about this, are you?" Julie asked, reading Dar's facial expression. "Really Dar, you're making too much of this. We just saw a movie. It was nothing."

Dar did not respond. She couldn't. Anger blocked her throat and made her speechless. Her mind could barely rationalize her feelings. On the one hand, she wasn't prepared to accuse Julie of going after Marc unless she knew for sure exactly what Julie's motives were. On the other hand, she knew Julie well.

She knew that this was precisely the kind of game Julie was capable of playing, and what was more disconcerting, winning. And, if Julie was playing a game, was she doing it just to mess with Dar? Or was she really serious about Marc?

Dar did not know the answer to any of these questions. The fact that she did not know, the fact that she was not sure of Julie's motives, made Dar feel like Julie had the upper hand. Dar could not be sure of the truth. That made her feel powerless, which in turn, made her feel completely outraged.

Mr. Clark came in and started the class. Dar did not want to think about Marc and Julie together, but thoughts of them kept popping into her mind and disrupting her concentration.

Every time she thought about Marc and Julie going to the movies together, she felt like screaming.

*If it had been anyone else who had gone to the movies with Marc, would I feel the same way?* she wondered as Mr. Clark droned on. *What if it had been Ariel or Danni? Would I still be angry?*

She decided that she would feel angry if any of them had gone with Marc, even if it was just as friends. Still, she thought that her emotions were irrational and unjustified. If Julie had gone with Sean or Drew or anyone else, she would not have thought twice about it.

Dar and Julie left history class without saying another word to each other. The next three periods were torture for Dar, worse than the day before, if that were possible. No one had said anything to her about the rumor or about Sean so far that day, but then, Dar refused to even look at anyone, so no one had a chance. A few times she thought she heard comments from unseen faces uttered just loud enough for her to hear as she walked by. However, at this point, she did not care. Emotionally, she was ice.

She could not even warm up for Danni, who assumed Dar's iciness to be anger towards her from the day before.

"Honestly, Dar, I am so sorry about yesterday," Danni whispered to her during a moment of chaos in their chemistry class.

Dar shook her head from side to side. "Don't worry about it," she said without really looking at Danni. It was not exactly a statement of forgiveness, but it was all Dar had in her at the moment. Danni continued to look as upset and as guilty as she did before.

*I'll call her later and apologize,* Dar thought, noting Danni's upset demeanor. But after a moment's consideration, Dar's sense of compassion got the better of her. She decided to put Danni's mind at ease.

"I'm not mad at you," she said. "I've just got a lot on my mind."

"Yesterday must have been really awful for you," Danni sympathized.

"It wasn't fun," Dar conceded. She so wanted to tell Danni what was going on between her and Julie, but she instinctively knew that telling Danni would only make things worse. Danni would never think badly of Julie no matter what Dar said. Telling her would only complicate the situation. Dar stopped herself from speaking any further.

Chemistry came to an end. Danni stood up to leave. "Dar, I'm truly sorry about yesterday," she said. "I'll text you later." Then, she left for her next class.

Dar procrastinated getting up. She sat like a lump in her seat. Finally, she picked up her books and headed towards Spanish.

Dar walked slowly thinking about Elyse Serano, who she would be seeing in just a few minutes. She felt sure that Elyse had heard the rumor about her and Sean Parker. Elyse's attitude had certainly changed towards her. Now, on top of everything else, Dar had to deal with that.

It wasn't as though Elyse meant much more to Dar than someone to sit next to in Spanish class. But, she did like Elyse, and Elyse was a senior, and there was still another eight months left in the school year. It was going to be a long eight months if Dar continued to feel as uncomfortable as she did yesterday while sitting next to Elyse.

*Maybe at some point, I can have a private convo with her,* Dar thought. *Explain that nothing happened between me and Sean. It was just a rumor. Not today, though. Today is just about surviving.*

She decided to wait until the very last minute to

enter Spanish class. She moved slowly through the hallway. She reached the classroom and lingered just outside the door, waiting for the bell to ring. Then, just as Mrs. Delgado was pulling the door closed, Dar slipped inside. She immediately trained her eyes on Elyse's chair. It was empty. After all that, Elyse was absent. Dar felt relieved.

Dar sat in her Spanish class, doodling. She had given up trying to focus way back in history class. She wanted to talk with someone about Julie, but who? She could not very well talk to Danni or Ariel; they were too close to Julie. She did have other friends, acquaintances really, but she could not think of anyone whom she really trusted. Whomever she talked to would have to know Julie well, and there was no one other than their close mutual friends who really knew her. Perhaps Brit? Brit had been genuinely concerned for Dar yesterday. But she did not want to put Brit in the middle of a situation between herself and Julie. No, she would have to figure this out on her own.

Dar looked at the clock. Lunch was only forty minutes away. She was going to have to sit with Julie, Ariel, and Danni at lunch, just as she always did. It would be weird if she didn't. She was going to have to face Julie. She was going to have to act like everything was normal between them. Dar didn't think she could do that. She didn't want to do that. To act like everything was okay when it wasn't? What would she say? Could she even pretend to be civil for the sake of

Danni and Ariel? Dar did not think she could.

As the seconds ticked by, Dar began to feel a knot tightening in her stomach. She nearly groaned out loud from the increasing tension and nausea. There was not going to be any need for lunch at this rate.

*Maybe I should go to the nurse's office instead?* she considered. *I could lie down for a while. I could stay through lunch and p.e. I would not have to see Julie for the rest of the day. I might be avoiding my problems, but so what?*

By the time Spanish class had come to an end, Dar had made up her mind that she was going to escape to the nurse's office. She did not want to see Julie. She did not want to see Ariel or Danni or anyone else. She did not want to face the social pressures of the cafeteria. She did not want to hear any more gossip about her and Sean. She had had all she could take.

Dar exited her Spanish class hoping to be able to sneak by everyone she knew. The nurse's office was not far away, just down the hall and to the right. But she had to walk in the opposite direction from the cafeteria. She was nearly trampled by hordes of kids, racing to lunch. She managed to slide along the hallway wall until she reached the door to the nurse's office. Once there, she ducked inside.

The school nurse, Mrs. Bradford, was a kind and smiley woman in her late 40's. She took her job seriously. No matter how many kids came through her doors (some faking illnesses, some truly sick), she treated each one with solicitous care and doting attention. Dar knew that she would have no trouble convincing Mrs. Bradford that she did not feel well.

Mrs. Bradford looked up from her paperwork with a concerned expression on her face as Dar entered.

"What can I do for you, Darlene?" she asked.

"I was wondering if I could lie down for a little while?" Dar responded. "I have an upset stomach and a bit of a headache."

Since kids rarely pick lunchtime to fake an illness, Mrs. Bradford was sure that Dar was truly sick. She felt Dar's forehead, and although it was cool to the touch, she asked, "Do you want to go home?"

"No. I think if I just lay down through lunch and my E period p.e. class, I will be okay. I really don't want to miss my math class during F period."

Sympathetic to Dar's conscientious concern for her math class, Mrs. Bradford agreed to allow Dar to lie down through the end of E period. She promised to wake Dar up for her math class if she fell asleep.

Dar was somewhat relieved that Mrs. Bradford had accepted her excuse. However, she was little comforted by the arrangement. It was true that she would not have to face Julie for the rest of the day, but she spent the entire time worrying about what Julie might think when she did not show up for lunch or p.e.

*Will Julie be mad at me? Will she understand just how angry I am? Will she take it personally, or just shrug it off? Will she talk to Ariel and Danni about me?*

Dar lay in the nurse's office, trying to relax her mind to no avail. Thoughts about Julie and Marc bombarded her brain.

*Will Julie be seeing Marc again today?* she wondered.

She wanted to believe that the jaunt to the movies meant nothing to either of them. But the thought of them together, maybe at Julie's house later today, made her feel jealous, rejected, and left out.

Dar lay there trying to make sense of her feelings. She could not shake the gut feeling that Julie had set her up, that she had done this to her on purpose.

*Why don't I trust her?* she wondered.

And then, the question that Dar had been avoiding for the last twenty-four hours, that niggling question that she had crushed and tamped down, the question that she had successfully denied existence to up until now, came exploding up out of the depths of her subconscious mind like a million tons of water breaking through a dam. It flooded every corner of her awareness; it demanded every inch of her attention. *Could it have been Julie that started the rumor about me and Sean? Did she set me up to sabotage me and Marc?*

Dar shuddered at the idea. She quickly pushed it out of her mind. She did not want to think the worst of her best friend. *I am making too much of this*, she told herself. *Marc and Julie barely know each other. It really was nothing.* But she could not quite convince herself of that.

She lay there wishing that none of this had happened, that Julie had not gone with Marc so that she and Julie could go back to being best friends. She wished, too, that a rumor had not been started about her and Sean. She wished that her life could magically go back to the way it was just twenty-four hours ago. Normally, she would have been looking forward to lunch with the *G Girls*. It was always a welcome chill-moment in the middle of the day. But Julie had gone with Marc behind her back, and now, regardless of whether Julie's intentions were innocent or not, Dar had to decide if she was going to forgive her.

Dar lay there counting the seconds until the end of E period. Each second was agony. She wasn't sure if she wanted E period to end. She wanted the school day to be over, but she dreaded having to leave the security of the nurse's office.

At 1:25 p.m., Dar got up. She texted her mother to let her know that she would need a ride home from school. Then, she used the restroom in the nurse's office. She applied fresh lipstick and blush. She fixed her hair so that it didn't look like she had just gotten out of bed. She asked Mrs. Bradford for a glass of water, hoping that that would perk her up.

"How are you feeling?" Mrs. Bradford asked.

"A little better," Dar lied.

The bell rang. Dar walked through the halls

carefully. She was far enough away from the gym to be fairly certain that her path would not cross any of her friends. Still, she felt a little anxious as she moved through the hallways. If she could just get through the rest of the day without seeing Julie or any of them, she would be okay. Once at home, she would be able to lock herself away in the security of her own room. She would be able to relax, let down her guard, and sort through this whole mess. A night away from everyone would give her time and enough distance to gain perspective. Her thoughts and feelings would become clear. She would know what to do then.

Dar stealthily reached the door to her classroom. She ducked inside. She breathed a sigh of relief. *I made it,* she thought. *The last class of the day, and then, I can go home.*

She turned to take her seat. There was Julie. She was seated on top of Dar's desk, her feet dangling over the edge. A little smirk graced her lovely face. She had her back to Robert Ferrier who was eyeing her with outright revulsion.

Dar quickly prepared herself for a confrontation. She squared her shoulders. She headed straight for Julie. *No use resisting now,* she thought.

"We missed you at lunch and p.e.," Julie began as Dar came towards her. "Where were you?"

"In the nurse's office. I had a headache," Dar said flatly. Her tone clearly signaled that she did not want to speak to Julie.

Julie paused momentarily, assessing Dar's demeanor. "Dar, I know you're mad at me," she said finally. "But really, you don't need to be. It was innocent. Nothing happened."

"Why don't I believe you?" Dar asked, dropping her book bag heavily onto a nearby desk and crossing her arms.

"Dar, I'm insulted. You know you're fam. You know I would never go after a guy you were interested in," Julie said, gently reassuring her.

Dar clenched her jaw. *Do I?* she thought.

As Dar continued to stare at Julie, she began to feel herself soften inwardly. Outwardly, Dar maintained a stone-cold look on her face. But after a few seconds, she involuntarily dropped her shoulders. She looked down at the floor. It was a gesture of confusion and defeat. She observed how quickly Julie could win her over, and she didn't like it. *I'm giving in to her too easily,* Dar thought.

Julie sensed she was making progress. "Come on, Dar," she coaxed. "We missed you at lunch," she repeated. "Come to my house after school today. Marc will be there," Julie said, dangling the final carrot. But instead of being the enticement that Julie had hoped for, the promise of seeing Marc caused Dar to explode.

"I don't want to see him," she hissed. "I suppose Sean will be there too. I can't face either of them. Especially not together."

Julie looked surprised. This was not at all the

reaction she had been expecting. "Wha . . . how come?" she asked.

"Because. What if Marc's into you now? What if he likes you? I don't want to hang around while he curves me and goes after you.

"Or what if he heard the rumor about me and Sean? What if he thinks I hooked up with Sean? He won't speak to me, and I will be mortified.

"And," Dar continued. "I don't want to see Sean either. After he started a rumor about me and him? I can't hang out with him as if nothing happened. If I see him, I'm going to go off on him."

For once, Julie was silent. The situation was so much more complicated than either of them had realized. There was a pause in the exchange. They both instinctively looked at the clock on the wall. The bell was about to ring. They had only a few seconds to conclude their conversation.

Dar took a deep breath. "I'm just going home after school today," she said wearily with a hint of regret in her voice. "Maybe we can do something tomorrow," she conceded.

Julie nodded hopefully. "You promise?" she asked.

"I'll think about it," Dar said. She wasn't ready to commit just yet.

Julie hopped off the desk taking Dar's response as a "yes." She quickly vanished out the classroom door.

Dar dropped heavily into her seat. She carelessly

took out her algebra book, some scrap paper, and a pencil. Mr. Reed was taking his time starting the class, so she had a moment to breathe.

Robert leaned forward in his chair. "What's going on?" he asked nosily.

"Oh nothing," Dar said dismissively. As sweet as Robert was, she was not about to discuss the details of her personal life with him. But Robert would not drop it.

"Whatever Julie tells you, don't believe her. She's a master manipulator. I don't know what she's up to, what her game is, but I bet you she has one. I don't know how you two can be best friends. You're so nice, and she's, you know, evil."

Dar wished Robert would shut up, but instead he continued.

"In case you hadn't noticed, Dar, Julie is a bee-ee-ee-ee-ee-yaah-chee." Robert stretched out each syllable of the word, bouncing on the ee's while making a face that made him look like he had just seen something horrific, and it was painful for him to speak.

Dar giggled at his weird theatrics. She paused for a second. Then she said, "I know. That's what makes her so special to me."

They both laughed.

∆∆∆

Mrs. Blaise was waiting when Dar exited the school at 2:35 p.m. Dar was relieved to see her. She was grateful that her mother was on time, grateful that she did not run into any of her friends on the way out of the building, and grateful to get away from the school altogether. She opened the car door, tossed her backpack into the back seat, and climbed in next to her mother.

"This is an unexpected treat," her mother said as they pulled away from the curb. "I can't remember the last time you came home after school two days in a row. Is everything okay?" she asked.

"Everything is fine. Julie's mother still doesn't feel well," Dar said with conviction. "And don't get used to it," she warned.

Mrs. Blaise laughed. "Okay. Don't worry. I'm a mother, not delusional. But since you're here, and since it is a treat for me, let's go for ice cream before your sisters come home."

"Sure," Dar said. She was hungry from missing lunch. "But I'll have to go for a run afterwards."

"Fine. Do whatever you feel you need to," her mother said. "Just don't expect me to come with."

They drove fifteen minutes out of town to their favorite ice cream stand adjacent to a local dairy farm. Dar ordered a vanilla milkshake. Her mother got two scoops of ice cream, peach and raspberry, on a wafer cone. They sat side-by-side at one of the picnic tables facing the pasture, and watched the cows.

It was a cool but sunny October day with open blue skies. They talked about Dar's classes, about Halloween coming up, about her sisters, and about nothing at all. Dar felt herself relax as she fell into the familiar ease of being with her mother. She traded her anxiety and worry for safety and trust.

They finished up their ice cream and hung out a little longer, both enjoying the sunshine and the break from the usual routine. Finally, they got back into their car and headed for home. They arrived just in time to meet the school bus and greet Dar's sisters.

As soon as she entered the house, Dar went straight to her room to change her clothes. She had been spending so many afternoons with her friends that she barely had time to go for a run now that the days were getting shorter. Today she had a reason to run, and it wasn't just to work off the milkshake. She needed to get away from the commotion of her household; she needed time by herself and she needed to release the emotions that she had been holding in all day long.

The Blaises lived in a neighborhood not far from a park called "Arrowhead River Trails." At the entrance to the park, two small rivers merged to form a third river. Dar's favorite run was a four-mile route that took her through the park and along the trail that ran parallel to the river. The trail was about a half mile stretch of land with the Arrowhead River on one side and fields of wildflowers on the other.

She told her mother that she would be back in

an hour and headed off. She ran the mile and a half to the park, and then picked up the dirt trail. She pounded along the trail, one foot in front of the other, concentrating on maintaining a steady pace.

She was three quarters of the way through the park before her mind began to drift back to the events of the day. Every time she thought about Julie, every time she imagined Julie asking Marc to go to the movies with her, every time she thought about the casual way in which Julie had dropped that bomb on her during history class as if it were nothing, Dar felt a surge of anger. And every time she felt a surge of anger, Dar ran harder.

Even the way Julie had just shown up in Dar's math class, wanting Dar to forgive her, wanting everything to go back to normal, acting as if the events of the last few days had not happened at all - even that bugged Dar.

*Did Julie even apologize? No, she didn't. She just asserted that there was nothing to apologize for, that she had done nothing wrong. Well, maybe Julie didn't intentionally do anything wrong. Maybe she just didn't think.*

It would have been just like Julie to ask Marc to go to the movies without thinking about how Dar might feel. Julie was used to doing whatever she wanted. If she were bored, she would have seen the arrival of Marc as an opportunity to get out of the house. Even if she flirted with Marc, it would not necessarily have meant anything. Julie flirted with lots of guys – except guys like Robert Ferrier - guys she did not deem worthy.

Dar reached the end of the trail. The wind picked up a little. The cool air kept her from getting too warm. It felt good. Sunset was still an hour away. She had plenty of time before darkness set in. She turned around.

As she started the run back, Dar began to reflect upon the history of her relationship with Julie.

They had become friends in the seventh grade when they both sat near Mike Kessler and Ryan Hall in humanities class. The four of them used to fool around mercilessly, to the point where Mrs. Davis had to separate their seats.

Julie invited Dar to her sleep-over birthday party that year, and that's when their friendship really began. They went to their first middle school formal dance and to their first boy-girl party together. Back then, Dar and Julie were popular for sure, but so were lots of other kids. Their friend-group was wide. The main goal was to have fun. Games, music, styles, movies, vids, memes, trends of all sorts, were all part of the adventure.

So, what happened? Eighth grade changed everything. Julie came back from summer vacation on a mission. Little by little, she began to exclude one girl after another from their circle of friends. She became the sole determiner of who was in and who was out.

She began to hang around with Jeff and his

friends, at first by herself, and then later inviting select girls to join her. She started going out with Damon Johnston. She was constantly posting pictures of the two of them together. And by the time she entered high school, Juliette Lyons had established herself as the leader of the *G Girls*.

Dar thought about how Julie had carefully whittled down their friend-group to just the *G Girls*; how she had made it subtly uncomfortable for the girls she wanted to exclude to be around her. Little criticisms, comments, subtle insults, ignoring, shaming, injury by a thousand little cuts barely noticeable, until the unwitting victim decided that it was too painful and too humiliating for her to be around Julie and her friends.

Dar witnessed Julie's tactics again and again without really caring. As a frosh, Dar derived strength from the group's strong identity and close relationships. She did not care about the kids they left behind. In fact, life was easier without them. She was having fun, life was exciting, and that was just how the game was played. She was in high school now. Everyone was sorting themselves into smaller, tighter groups. Everyone was defining their identities - accepting some and rejecting others - not just she and Julie.

Besides, no matter what Julie did, Dar had always felt secure in their friendship. Although lately, Dar found herself becoming more and more irritated with Julie's self-proclaimed authority, and her need to control Dar's every decision. A tension had developed between them. Maybe Julie was feeling threatened by Dar's growing sense of independence and her desire to make her own choices? Maybe it was Dar's turn to be whittled from their group?

Dar slowed her pace to barely a jog. She came upon a bench and sat down. She surveyed the expanse of straw-colored field before her, landing her eyes on a very mellow, late fall sun. The sun was just threatening to drop behind the stark, black treeline. The breeze was gentle and soft. It felt good in her nose and on her skin.

Dar let out a sigh. She looked down at her feet. She wished that she could stay out there forever. Instead, she would have to settle for just a few more minutes - a few more minutes of serenity, of pure, sensuous mindlessness before she started the final jog back, back to the world of family and homework, and facing the future, and pretending to everyone that everything was okay.

On the last leg of the run, Dar thought about Robert Ferrier. Dar had never seen Robert so vehemently angry before. She had never heard him say anything bad about anyone before. She wondered what Julie had done to him, aside from dismissing his very existence. He clearly hated her and possibly with good reason.

*The beautiful, exciting, powerful, and slightly-twisted Juliette Lyons,* Dar thought as she listened to the steady, rhythmic pounding of her feet. *Boys want to be with her; girls want to be her; girls are jealous, but still want to hang with her. But,* she wondered, *does anyone actually like her?*

# THURSDAY MORNING
## CHAPTER 5

They were both waiting for her when she entered her history class the next day, not just Julie, but Sean and Julie. Dar looked from one to the other and immediately realized that she was out-numbered and about to be out-maneuvered.

"Dar, I know you're mad at me, but hear me out," Julie started.

*At least she's figured that out. At least she's figured out that I'm pissed at her. That's a little progress,* Dar thought.

Julie continued.

"So yesterday, Sean and I were hanging with Marc and Jeff, and we brought up the rumor. Marc hadn't heard it. So we told him what kids were saying about you and Sean and about how it was all untrue. So now Marc knows that nothing happened. And Sean is here -"

"I don't know why you didn't want to fake hook up

with me, Dar," Sean interrupted, slightly pouting. "We could have fake had a good time together."

"You're not helping, Sean." Julie glared at him.

"Anyway, now you have nothing to worry about. Marc knows the truth, and Sean's here, so there's no reason to avoid hanging out with us."

Dar turned to Sean. "Promise me you will stop telling people that we hooked up?" she demanded.

"Hey, I did not start that rumor," Sean said, practically yelling at her. "I never told anyone that. Give me a little credit for having some integrity. Although, I can't pretend that I didn't enjoy the rep, just a little."

"'Not helping!" Julie told him.

"Well, promise me that you will set people straight if they bring it up. It's been a nightmare for me. I have never been so humiliated," Dar said.

"Hey! I have feelings too, you know," Sean asserted.

Dar wasn't sure if Sean was joking or serious.

"Of course you do," she said with just a touch of sarcasm. Then, she added, "I'm sorry. It's not a personal thing. So, promise me you will set people straight, okay?"

"Okay. Yes. Of course. I promise," Sean said.

"So we're good?" Julie asked.

"Well, I think Sean and I are good," Dar affirmed. She wanted Julie to sweat it out just a little longer.

She had to admit, though, that Julie had gone out of her way to rectify the situation, and that was unlike her in every respect.

"And us?" Julie asked, looking at Dar. She patiently waited for the answer she wanted.

Dar was still not ready to flat-out say "yes." Instead, she tilted her head to one side as if in thought. Then, she barely nodded in agreement. That was enough for Julie.

"Sweet. Awesome." Julie's face brightened.

"Can I go?" Sean asked.

"Yes, and don't get into any more trouble," Julie called after him as he disappeared out of the door. She turned back to Dar.

"So, what are you doing later today?" she asked.

And although Dar agreed to meet up with Julie and the girls that afternoon, she still felt slight pangs of distrust and a little uneasy about the whole thing.

$$\triangle\triangle\triangle$$

First period history class came to an end. Dar was glad. She packed up her stuff and said goodbye to Julie. She hurried off to the library for study hall, her only study hall of the week.

Arriving early, she put her book bag down on a table in the back of the room. She pulled out the novel she was reading. She had nothing else to do but escape into a book for fifty minutes. She could use the break.

Dar had barely made it through one page when Damon Johnston, the former boyfriend of Julie and the current boyfriend of Carrie Ellis, arrived. He dropped his math book onto the table. He carelessly tossed a pencil on top of it. He pulled back the chair next to Dar's and sat down.

Dar looked up from her book. "Hey," she said gently.

Dar closed her book. She turned to face Damon. Having been distracted by her own problems all week, she had forgotten all about Carrie Ellis. She had forgotten about the fight at the dance and about the fact that she had been looking forward to finding out what actually happened between Carrie Ellis and Teresa Manning.

"How are you? How's Carrie doing?" Dar asked Damon, not waiting for him to start the conversation.

"Terrible. It's been a nightmare," he replied, his voice heavy with emotion. "Worse than you can imagine."

"Oh no!" Dar responded. She hadn't expected such a dire tone. "What's going on?" she asked.

"Well, Carrie was at the dance on Saturday night," Damon started.

Dar wanted to interrupt to tell him that she already knew Carrie had been in a fight, but she stopped herself. *Better let him tell me the whole story from the beginning,* she thought.

"I wasn't there. My parents made me go to a family thing. Anyway, Carrie was standing on the dance floor with some friends when Teresa Manning came up behind her. Teresa put her arm around Carrie's neck. She pulled her backward in a choke hold. Then, she put her mouth right up against Carrie's ear and said, 'Stay away from my man, bitch!'"

"Wait," Dar stopped him. "Who's Teresa's 'man'? Did she mean you?"

"Ach! No! I have no idea," Damon answered. "I can assure you it is not me. I have never even spoken to the girl. I couldn't have picked her out from among a herd of elephants before all this happened. She's so hideous. I'm sure no guy in this school would touch her."

"I'm sorry. Keep going," Dar said. All of her attention was focused on Damon. She held her breath, waiting to hear the rest of the story.

"It's possible that Teresa was planning to just threaten Carrie and let her go, but Carrie panicked. She went crazy. She elbowed Teresa in the gut. She kicked backwards, catching Teresa in the shin and causing her to lose her balance. Teresa started to fall, but instead of letting go of Carrie, she tightened her hold. The two of them went down together. Carrie was screaming. Teresa was behind her, still holding her neck. Teresa tried to roll over and get on top of

Carrie, but she didn't have control of Carrie's arms. Carrie was swinging wildly. She hit Teresa's nose. She must have hit her hard because Teresa let go. That's when the teachers were able to jump in.

"Somebody pulled the two of them apart – Carrie's not sure who. She was still swinging wildly. One of the teachers grabbed her arms and held her until the police arrived. They handcuffed both Teresa and Carrie. They dragged them out of the gym and put them into patrol cars.

"At first Carrie was crying hysterically, but when the policeman put his hand on her head and pushed her down into the car, she went into shock. She couldn't speak. It all happened so fast. One minute, she was in the DHS gym, talking with friends, the next minute, she was in a police car in handcuffs.

"They took Teresa to the hospital for her nose, and they took Carrie to the police station. Thankfully, she never saw Teresa Manning again. Once they got Carrie into the police station, they booked her, fingerprinted her, took mugshots of her, and put her in a holding cell all by herself. They didn't even give her an opportunity to call her parents. She didn't know how long they were going to keep her there. She didn't know if they were going to keep her all night or if anyone was going to call her parents for her."

"Oh my God! She must have been terrified! I would have been throwing up," Dar said.

"I know, right? I would have been throwing up too,"

Damon agreed.

He took a deep breath and swallowed hard. He looked down at the table, fighting back tears. Dar could see that he was trying to compose himself. She waited patiently. She felt badly for him. She wanted to reach out and touch his hand sympathetically, but she wasn't sure how he would receive it. She could see how deeply he had been affected by all of this.

Damon suddenly looked up and resumed speaking.

"Fortunately, Mr. Andrews, the vice principal - thank God for that guy – he had enough sense to get in his car and follow the police down to the station. He called Carrie's parents, and he stayed at the station until they arrived. He waited with them until the police released Carrie into their custody. But the police made Carrie and her parents wait a long time before she could go home. She didn't get home until after 1:00 a.m. A judge had to set bail and approve her release which was why it took so long, I guess.

"Whoa! That's crazy!" Dar was stunned. It never occurred to her that Carrie would have been put through so much; that she would have been treated like a violent criminal.

"But that's not the worst part," Damon said.

*How can that not be the worst part?* Dar wondered.

"I mean, it's terrible to be attacked; it's humiliating to be taken out of the gym in handcuffs in front of the whole school, and it's terrifying to be arrested and jailed. But the worst part is that now Carrie has a criminal record. She was charged with assault, disorderly conduct, and resisting arrest! Can you imagine Carrie committing assault? She's like the sweetest, most gentle person in the whole world."

Damon's characterization of Carrie was a bit exaggerated, of course, but Dar had to agree that the idea of Carrie Ellis doing any of those things was ludicrous. She had clearly been victimized by Teresa Manning, and now she was being punished for defending herself.

Damon continued. "She's been suspended for three weeks. She has to appear in court. They're probably going to make her go for counseling. She will be put on probation. Hopefully, they won't send her to a juvenile detention facility, but her lawyer says they could. Most likely, she'll have to report to a probation officer every week. And, she won't be able to leave the state.

"But here's the very worst part: it will be on her permanent record. It could ruin her chances of getting into college, at least into a top tier school. And you know how serious Carrie is about getting into a top tier school. She works so hard to keep up her grades. She's ranked second in the sophomore class, you know," he said proudly.

Dar wasn't surprised by this last statement. She knew Carrie to be very quiet and very studious. *I wonder who is ranked first?* she thought randomly.

Damon continued. "I have been to see her every day this week. I have been trying to cheer her up, but she's in such a state. She feels as if her life is over. She doesn't want to go back to school. . . ever. She won't even leave the house. Her parents are really worried about her, too. They've spoken to the school psychologist, who thinks she should be put on suicide watch."

Damon stopped talking abruptly. He looked down at his hands. Dar thought he looked depressed, worn-out from worrying, and a little sad. It had been a trauma for him too.

*If Carrie doesn't come out of this, they'll probably break up*, she thought involuntarily. *No guy in high school is going to stay with someone who's situation is so complicated for very long – no matter how much he cares about her.*

"Poor Carrie," Dar said softly. "I had no idea."

All of Dar's interest had been in finding out what had happened at the dance. She wanted to know all the juicy details. She hadn't considered what Carrie might be feeling or facing in the least. She remembered the embarrassment and humiliation that she had endured during the past few days. Her own troubles were nothing compared to Carrie's. Dar's problems would pass, but Carrie's were just beginning. Carrie's life, her future - the future she had worked for, the future she had planned for, the future she had envisioned for herself - was now in ruins.

△△△

The rest of the day passed by slowly like an ant making its way through bubble gum. Dar ate lunch with her friends, now that she and Julie had reconciled. It wasn't like she had consciously decided to forgive Julie; she simply found it useless to be angry with her. It just made more sense for Dar to resume living her life. If Ariel and Danni were aware that she and Julie had been fighting, they did not show it. Everything seemed normal, at least on the surface.

Dar was quiet, though. She half-heartedly joined in the conversation with her friends as they inanely discussed which one of them would make a better rideshare driver. They all thought that Julie would be the fastest, but also the most reckless. Julie thought that she would be the best at getting through traffic, and that Ariel would be the most likely to get lost, even with GPS. Ariel thought that the passengers in her car would have the most fun, and therefore, she would get the biggest tips. They all agreed that Danni would be the slowest and that Dar would be the safest as well as the most likely to always know where she was going. It should have been a fun conversation, but Dar felt unconsciously, almost imperceptibly, weighed down. She had been through a lot since Monday, and she wasn't quite prepared to let it all go, as much as she wished she could.

Talking to Damon had been heavy. Carrie's life was not Dar's problem. She barely knew the girl. And yet, she could not help but feel the weight of Carrie's situation burdening her own life. She had experienced an inkling of how brutal and how mean people could be; how unthinking and how cruel. It wasn't that easy to blithely move on from it all.

*How fast everything can change!* she thought. *High school should be fun. Not all this seriousness!*

But the burden of reality and consequence felt as if it were breathing down her neck.

# THURSDAY AFTERNOON
## CHAPTER 6

The afternoon plan was to head to Java Palooza, the local hipster coffee bar. The girls intended to study there. Dar and Julie had a history exam the next day, Danni had a math quiz, and Ariel had to write a two-page paper on a novel that she hadn't even finished reading. Julie's brother Jeff dropped them off after school.

The girls entered the cafe. They ordered their iced teas and frappuccinos. They found a large, empty table and deposited their backpacks. They pulled out computers, phones, and notebooks. They spread their study materials all over the flat surface. They went back to pick up their drinks. After a few minutes of relaxing and catching up with each other, they got to work.

Every five minutes or so, they interrupted each other with a joke, a comment, or a question. They had collectively perfected the art of conversing while studying. Julie and Dar were particularly good at engaging in banter as they pored over their history notes. Danni intermittently joined in between algebra problems, and Ariel periodically looked up from her book just long enough to give them all a dirty look.

For the first time since Monday, Dar was enjoying being with her friends. She had felt hesitant when she agreed to meet them after school, but the dual conditions of having to study plus the neutrality of a coffee shop turned out to be just what she needed to ease back in.

"You're awfully quiet over there," Julie said, focusing on Ariel.

"I just want to get this done," Ariel replied.

"It must be a good book," Julie said.

"I don't know how anyone can think *Lord of the Flies* is a good book. I had to read it last summer," Danni interjected.

"It's gross," Ariel said, not offering more than that. She returned to her reading.

"Gross?" Julie sounded surprised.

"Yes, gross. Boys hunting boys. Gross," she said.

"'Survival of the fittest' or 'man's inhumanity to man' - which is it?" Danni asked.

"Maybe 'men are pigs'? Literally!" Ariel replied.

Danni giggled.

"What about girls?" Dar asked.

"Girls are pigs?" Danni asked.

"No, not 'girls are pigs'," Dar clarified, "girls hunting girls."

There was a pause in the conversation as Julie, Danni, and Ariel eyed Dar with curiosity and mild concern.

"That's kind of a dark thought, Dar," Julie said. "Are you feeling okay?"

Dar took a moment to consider what she herself had just said.

"I don't know. Maybe I'm not," she said slowly. "I was just thinking of Teresa Manning going after Carrie Ellis." She hadn't intended to bring up the subject, but there it was.

"Oh, that," Ariel said. "That's not the same thing. This is a book about a gang of boys who get stranded on an island and start hunting each other. It's not as if a gang of girls set out to make Carrie Ellis their prey. Carrie just got into a random fight with Teresa Manning at the school dance."

"I agree. It's not the same thing," Dar said, "but Teresa did go after Carrie Ellis on purpose. It wasn't entirely random."

"I know that's what Cindy Farr said, but I'm not sure I believe her," Ariel countered.

"It's true. I talked to Damon today," Dar said. She tried to gauge Julie's reaction to the mention of Damon's name.

Ariel put down her book. The three of them stared pointedly at Dar.

"What did he say?" Ariel prodded.

"Well, he said that Teresa did intentionally attack Carrie at the school dance. Teresa accused Carrie of going after her boyfriend."

"Wha? That's crazy!" Ariel said.

"That's what I said," Dar responded.

"Crazy that Teresa Manning has a boyfriend," Ariel continued. "Who would go out with her?"

"I have no idea," Dar answered.

"Doesn't Teresa know that Carrie already has a boyfriend?" Danni asked.

"I guess not," Dar answered.

"So, did Carrie really break Teresa's jaw?" Julie asked.

"No, her nose," Dar clarified. "It's not funny, though. Carrie is in a lot of trouble. She's going to have a permanent police record. Damon says she's very, very depressed - possibly suicidal."

"That's a bit exaggerated, don't you think?" Julie commented.

"I think she must be really scared," Dar said quietly.

ΔΔΔ

They all went back to studying.

Around 4:20, Danni closed her book. "My mom is coming at 4:30," she said. "Ariel, do you want a ride?"

"Sure," Ariel responded. She had finished reading the novel and was now playing with her laptop. "I hate writing papers," she said. "I'm going to have to do the rest of this assignment at home locked in my room."

Ariel closed her computer. She and Danni packed up their things. They cleaned up their mess and got ready to leave. Seconds later, they all spotted Mrs. Lucci pulling up to the curb in front of Java Palooza. The two girls hurried out the door, leaving Dar and Julie behind.

Dar and Julie continued to work. They had gone through nearly all of their notes as well as the three textbook chapters pertaining to tomorrow's test. It had taken them longer than it should have because of the many interruptions they had both enjoyed, but now they were intent on finishing up.

They were making their way through the very last list of terms for the test. They were almost finished when Julie put down her pen. She leaned back in her chair. She gathered up her hair with both hands, lifted it up onto the top her head, then let it fall behind her shoulders.

"I don't feel sorry for Carrie Ellis," she said out of the blue.

"I didn't think you would, considering that you hate her guts," Dar responded, looking up from her notes.

"I don't hate her guts," Julie said.

"Oh really? Frosh year you practically burned a hole through her with your demon stares every time she walked by you. You're jealous of the fact that she and Damon worked out, and you and Damon didn't." Dar was surprised by her own blunt response, but Julie just ignored her.

"'Think they'll break up after this?" Julie asked.

Dar shrugged. "It's possible. He seemed pretty upset today."

Julie leaned forward again. "I don't know for sure that this is what really happened. I'm not saying that it did," she began measuredly, "but Teresa Manning may have overheard me telling Brit that Carrie Ellis had a crush on Curt Frasier, and that Carrie was going to break up with Damon for Curt."

"Who is Curt Frasier?" Dar asked, not getting the picture.

"Curt Frasier is the guy that Teresa Manning likes," Julie responded.

"Wait, you told Brit that Carrie was interested in Teresa's boyfriend? In front of Teresa?"

"Not in front of Teresa. She may have overheard me, though."

"Oh my God! Julie!" Dar exclaimed, drawing back in shock.

"Well, how was I supposed to know it was going to lead to all this?" Julie asked. "I didn't know Teresa

Manning was going to go into high gear whack mode on Carrie Ellis."

"Julie, seriously? You know what Teresa Manning is capable of. Maybe you didn't know exactly what she would do, but you knew she was going to do something. You were intentionally trying to create trouble for Carrie. Why else would you have said it?"

"I didn't plan to say it," Julie said defensively. "It just popped out."

Dar was now working her way towards outrage as the full understanding of Julie's confession settled in.

"What you did wasn't right, Julie. You ruined Carrie's life!" Dar said accusingly.

"Don't be so extra, Dar. I doubt that her life has been ruined," Julie retorted. "And even if it has been, I didn't do it. Teresa Manning did. Besides, you're supposed to be my best friend. You're supposed to be on my side, not Carrie's."

"I am your best friend, and I'm telling you - you went too far. I'm not going to tell anyone about this, but I don't think what you did was right."

"Well, I'm not okay with your position on this," Julie said. She was beginning to get upset too. "If you were truly my best friend you wouldn't be all high-key sympathetic to Carrie. And you would be happier for me."

"Happier? For what? It's not like you're going to get back with Damon because of this. Am I supposed to be happy because the life of a girl you don't like has been ruined?"

"Yes. You are. If you were truly my best friend, you would be."

"That's sick, Julie. Carrie Ellis didn't do anything to you other than go out with a guy you were already broken up with. I can't be happy for you because her future has been decimated."

Julie stopped talking. She closed her mouth hard. She stared at Dar, wide-eyed. Dar had never seen Julie look so completely wounded. It was shocking to see her look so vulnerable. Dar's heart softened seeing just how upset Julie was. Yet, she could not bring herself to say that what Julie had done was right. Dar could not pretend to think and feel differently than she did.

Julie stood up. She walked to the condiment bar. She picked up a plastic cup and poured herself a complimentary glass of water. When she returned, her face was composed as if nothing had happened.

"If you aren't with me on this," Julie said coldly. "I think our friendship is over."

Dar was stunned.

*Just like that? Julie can't be serious! After so many years, she's willing to end our friendship over this?*

It was tempting to capitulate, to just give in, to tell Julie that she was right. Of course, Julie meant more to her than Damon or Carrie. But the ultimatum was unfair. Why did Dar have to lie about what she really thought and how she truly felt? Why did she have to choose between her own sense of right and wrong and her friendship with Julie?

"And if you really cared about me, you wouldn't ask me to deny my own sense of right and wrong," Dar returned. "You wouldn't make me choose between you and what I think is right."

"Well, I don't understand how you can feel the way you do. I don't know how you can take the side of someone you're not even friends with over me."

"I'm not taking Carrie's side. I just don't think what you did was right." Dar wanted to scream the words.

*Why isn't Julie getting this?* She wondered. *Can she really not understand that this has nothing to do with the personal conflict between her and Carrie Ellis?*

"I'm sorry you feel that way, Dar," Julie concluded. "I'm sorry I told you. I'm sorry I confided in my best friend. Clearly, you no longer want to occupy that position in my life. It doesn't matter. I have other friends. Ariel and Danni will stick by me. And we're still the *G Girls.* And we're still the hottest squad at DHS!"

Dar gave a half smile at this. She always appreciated Julie's spirit. It was the thing she liked best about her. Immediately, tears welled up in Dar's eyes. She dropped her head and looked down. A single tear fell onto the table. She was sure Julie saw it. Dar turned her head away. She was stuck between her affection for her friend and her own sense of right and wrong. She could deny her own conscience, but it wasn't going to disappear. It would always be there, gnawing at her.

"I guess I'll call my mom, then," Dar recovered.

Now, it was Julie's turn to be stunned. No one else but Dar would have known that Julie was disappointed.

"We can talk about this in the morning," Dar said gently. "We'll figure it out. Just give me a night to sleep on it."

"I don't know why you need a night," Julie said, her blue eyes flashing with hurt.

"I just do," Dar said.

"Well, let me know when you've figured it out, Dar." And with that, Julie abruptly got up and exited the coffee shop, leaving Dar alone to wonder at her own unyielding stubbornness.

△△△

*Oh phooey!* Dar sighed to herself. *Another long, agonizing evening ahead!*

She was in the car with her mother, just ten minutes away from home. She had barely said "hello" to her mother before slipping into her own little world. She didn't even try to act normal. She didn't care. Her mother eyed her with curiosity but said nothing.

Dar didn't feel like talking, but she didn't feel like thinking either. She let her mind go blank. It had been a very long week, and it was almost over. She had gone through just about every emotion possible: excitement, elation, disappointment, embarrassment, humiliation, fear, anxiety, jealousy, anger, sadness, outrage, hurt, loss, and shock. Now, she felt numb - numb and deeply, deeply tired.

Dar went through the motions of her evening activities like a zombie with a to-do list. During a momentary pause in her math homework, she let her mind wander to her fight with Julie.

*It's Julie's fault. She shouldn't have baited Teresa Manning to go after Carrie Ellis. And she shouldn't have given me an ultimatum!*

And, there was the crux of the matter; Julie should not have given Dar an ultimatum. Of course, Julie should not have baited Teresa either. But she did, and there was no changing that. Julie was not going to apologize or feel bad about her actions. She seemed to be incapable of understanding that there were real consequences to the game she was playing; consequences that had impacted not just Carrie, but also Teresa, Damon, and Dar, and now through Dar, Julie herself.

Dar took a very deep breath. She could easily forgive Julie; forgive, forget, and move on. She could agree to disagree. She could even pretend that Julie was somehow not responsible, that Julie had not intended her little prank to end in such a horrible mess. But to be expected to flat out deny her own sense of right and wrong - even for a friend?

Dar quickly put the question out of her mind. She returned to her math problems. All she wanted to do was finish her homework – finish her homework, go to bed, and not think.

It was 8:45 p.m., and she was done. She washed her face and brushed her teeth. She slipped into some comfy pajamas. She did not check her phone as she normally would have before bed. If anyone had texted her, she did not want to know.

She was in bed by 9:30 p.m. She felt comfortable, warm, and safe there. Within minutes, she was asleep.

# FRIDAY
## CHAPTER 7

Dar vaguely heard her alarm off in the distance. She opened one eye, reached out, and shut it off. Then she allowed herself to drift back to sleep. Minutes passed. Slowly, the demands of the day began to seep into her awareness.

*Get up!* she told herself. *You need to get ready for school. Did I do all my homework? What am I wearing? Am I meeting Julie? Julie? Oh no, Julie!*

She rolled over and groaned. There was no avoiding her fate now. She was going to have to face Julie in a short while. Still, she put that awareness aside. She got up and started her morning routine.

It wasn't until Dar was in the car on her way to school that she realized she could no longer avoid thinking about Julie. She would be seeing her in just a few minutes.

Dar reviewed the situation as logically as she could. Julie was angry with her, yet Dar had not reached out to smooth things over. Julie had given her an ultimatum, yet Dar had not agreed to take Julie's side. She did not want to lose her friendship with Julie. So, what was she going to do? What could she do?

*"Not to decide is to decide,"* Dar quoted to herself randomly. *What does that even mean?* she wondered.

Dar marveled at her own state of calmness as she said goodbye to her mother and closed the car door.

*It's all up to Julie now,* she thought as she climbed the stairs. *I'm okay with myself, with what I think and what I feel. Julie can either accept that I don't agree with her, or I will move on.*

Dar practically shocked herself with this last thought, but there it was. There was no denying it. She had decided all right, just not consciously. She would not go against herself.

The history classroom was nearly empty when Dar arrived. She sat down and took out her study materials. She had ten minutes to do a quick review, to jog her memory from yesterday. She skimmed through her notes. It gave her something to focus on other than her own problems.

The bell rang. Julie flew into the classroom just as Mr. Clark was closing the door. She took her seat next to Dar's.

"Hey" Dar whispered. Dar was sure Julie heard her, yet Julie said nothing in return. She looked straight ahead and made it perfectly clear that she was ignoring Dar.

*So, this is the way it's going to be,* Dar thought. *Julie is not going to speak to me.*

The history test was unexpectedly difficult. It took Dar the full fifty minutes to complete. She was still working when the bell rang. Julie, however, jumped up immediately. She handed in her exam and took off without a word to Dar, not even so much as a glance in her direction. Dar's heart sank as she watched Julie disappear out the classroom door.

Dar slowly gathered up her things. She headed off to her next class. She decided along the way to keep with her policy of "not thinking," since that had been working for her up until now. If she started to think about what was going on between her and Julie, she might dissolve into a puddle of tears and end up in the nurse's office again.

*Don't think about it. Block it out of your mind,* she told herself. *Just go to class. Do what you have to do. Don't think.*

She made it through her English class okay. Dar had not spoken to anyone in that class since Tuesday, the day of the rumor. She had decided that the kids in her English class were not worth her time. She found no reason to change her decision now. She focused solely on the teacher for fifty minutes and then left without a word to anyone.

Chemistry class was a different matter, however. She would be seeing Danni there. She wasn't sure how much Danni knew about what was going on between her and Julie. *How much did Julie tell her?* Dar wondered. *Is Danni even going to be talking to me?*

She entered the chemistry classroom and took her seat. A moment later, Danni arrived.

"How was your history exam?" Danni asked as she dropped her things onto her desk.

*She's talking to me!* Dar thought. *That's a good sign.*

"It went okay," Dar answered. "It was hard, but I was prepared. How was your algebra quiz?"

"I haven't taken it yet," Danni told her. "It's next period. We also have a chemistry lab due next week."

"Oh no," Dar groaned. "And I have a Spanish test on Monday. Everything is coming due at once."

"That always happens," Danni said.

Mr. Shepherd entered. He began speaking to the class. Dar turned her attention away from Danni and to the front of the room. She settled back into her seat.

*So, Danni is acting pretty normal,* she thought. *I don't think she knows what's going on between me and Julie . . . yet. She will soon. Whatever happens, this is Julie's choice. It's up to Julie to explain this to Danni and Ariel. I'm not going to say anything to either of them.*

She certainly would not make Danni or Ariel choose between her and Julie, but she was pretty sure Julie was going to. *Oh well,* she thought. *Whatevs . . .*

△△△

Chemistry class came to an end. Dar said good-bye to Danni and headed on to her Spanish class. For the first time since Tuesday, that nightmare of a day, Dar would be seeing Elyse Serano.

*She probably still thinks I fooled around with Sean,* Dar thought.

Dar entered the classroom. Elyse was already in her seat, waiting for the class to start. Dar sat down next to her.

"Hey," Dar said.

"Hey," Elyse returned. "Dar, I'm so happy. I completed my early-decision college application this week. I uploaded it yesterday."

"Felicidades!" Dar said, congratulating Elyse in Spanish. She offered Elyse her knuckles in a quiet gesture of support. Elyse met them with her own, and the two of them shared a fist-bump as if they were clinking glasses of champagne together.

"I have been so stressed all week," Elyse said. "I didn't think I was going to be able to get the application done. I ended up giving myself a migraine."

"Is that why you weren't in school on Wednesday?" Dar asked.

"Yes. And now I have a whole bunch of homework to make up. But it was all worth it because I got the application done. Yay!" Elyse continued with her own little, private celebration.

"Well, if you want to get together this weekend, I can show you what you missed," Dar offered. "We have a test coming up on Monday."

"That would be great," Elyse responded. "Could we meet tomorrow at Java?"

"Sure," Dar agreed.

*Hey, look at me. I have a new Java Palooza study buddy*, Dar thought half-heartedly. She was happy to have something to do on the weekend, even if it was just studying with Elyse. At the same time, it made her a little sad to think that she would not be spending her weekend with Julie, Ariel, and Danni the way she normally would.

Dar was still feeling slightly uneasy about the Sean rumor. She wondered if Elyse had heard it?

"I thought you were mad at me on Tuesday," she said to Elyse.

"Mad at you?" Elyse asked with confusion.

"Yes. Unfortunately, there was a nasty rumor going around about me and Sean Parker. Do you know him?" Dar asked.

"Oh, yeah," Elyse said. "I saw the posts, but Sean said they weren't true."

"Really?" Dar asked. "I thought maybe it was Sean

who started the rumor."

"No," Elyse said. "He told everyone in second period English that it was all a lie."

*So, Sean really did not start that rumor,* Dar reflected, *I wonder . . .*

△△△

Lunchtime came. Dar dropped off her books at her locker and headed for the cafeteria. She felt anxiety seeping in with every step. She wanted to turn and run, to go hide in the library for half an hour, but her legs just kept moving her forward. She wasn't even that hungry – well, maybe just a little.

She entered the food line and picked out her lunch, a slice of pizza and a bottle of water. She paid the cashier and exited the line. She stood at the front of the cafeteria surveying the room for a place to sit.

Dar scanned the room. She saw Julie, Ariel, and Danni seated at a table towards the back. She hesitated. She wondered if she should sit with them.

*If Julie doesn't speak to me, it's going to be an awkward lunch,* she reasoned. *And who knows what she's told Danni and Ariel? What if none of them speak to me? What if they are rude? What if they are outright mean? That would be embarrassing and painful!*

Dar wasn't willing to take the risk. She looked

around the room for other options. She saw Brit and two other girls sitting with a bunch of boys from their class. She could sit with them, but it would be unusual for her to do so, and she really didn't want anyone asking her questions. She wasn't ready to trigger a cascade of gossip, rumor, and speculation about her situation. No, better to sit with someone outside their circle, someone who really didn't know Julie.

She surveyed the room again. Off to her left, she spotted two girls, Kristen Brandt and Haley Marsden. They were sitting by themselves. Kristen had been Dar's lab partner in biology the year before. They had functioned well together as lab partners, but had not spent any time together outside of bio. There was no need for it. Dar had her group of friends and Kristen had hers.

*Sitting with Kristen is a definite option*, she thought. *It will probably be uncomfortable, but I can get through it.*

Dar approached the table as casually as she could. Her intention was to just eat lunch and leave as quickly as possible. It really didn't matter to her if Kristen and Haley interacted with her at all. However, to her surprise, Kristen greeted her warmly.

"Hey Dar," Kristen said. "What's going on?"

"Nothing," Dar answered. "Can I eat with you guys today?" she asked, pulling out a chair.

"Sure," Kristen answered. "Where's Julie?" she asked reflexively.

"She's over there," Dar replied, nodding her head in Julie's direction.

"Oh," Kristen responded, her eyes widening a little. She glanced at Haley but said nothing.

The rest of the conversation consisted of nothing in particular. Kristen and Haley did most of the talking and mostly with each other. Dar got the feeling that they were showing off for her just a little. She didn't care. She focused on eating her pizza. She wanted to finish her lunch as quickly as possible. She wanted to get to the gymnasium early, before Julie, Ariel, and Danni arrived. She did not want to have to encounter the *G Girls* in the locker room.

Dar stood up before her last bite of pizza had been completely chewed. She picked up her plate and brought it to the depository. She returned to the table and grabbed her bottle of water. She said "good-bye" to Kristen and Haley and exited the cafeteria.

*They'll probably talk about me now*, she thought.

Dar headed towards the gym. She entered the locker room. There was no one in there, not even Miss Pond. The room was completely empty. *Okay, this is good*, she thought.

Dar quickly changed into a pair of athletic leggings and a sports bra for p.e. class. She kicked off her ballet flats and donned a pair of klutzy-looking cross trainers that were required for the class. She was ready to go.

Dar pulled open the massive double doors to the

gymnasium. The room was eerily quiet. There was no one in there; nothing but some thick, well-stacked wrestling mats, some basketball hoops, and a mass of ropes dangling from the ceiling.

At the start of each p.e. class, the students normally lined up against the wall opposite the double door entrance. Dar walked to the farthest corner of the gym, away from the double doors. She sat down on the floor and leaned back against the wall. She positioned herself so that she would be at the very end of the student line-up. She wanted to put as much distance as she possibly could between herself and the rest of the class.

Dar did not know what was going to happen during p.e. today. She did not know what fresh tortures were in store for her. She did not want a repeat of last Tuesday, if she could help it. And she wanted to avoid coming face-to-face with Julie, Ariel, and Danni. She knew that she was going to have to face them eventually. But not here, not today.

Dar occupied herself by humming her current favorite tune and inspecting her nail polish. *Time for another manicure*, she thought.

She moved on from her nails to her cross-trainers, stretching out her legs and looking at the shoes from various angles. She wondered if she should ask her mother for a new pair of shoes. She liked her running shoes so much better than these cross-trainers, but how much running did she really do in p.e. anyway? Not that much.

Dar sat patiently waiting for a full five minutes before the gym doors opened and Miss Pond, the p.e. teacher, entered. Miss Pond certainly looked surprised to see Dar sitting there.

"You're here early," Miss Pond said, coming towards her.

"Yup," Dar replied, offering no explanation.

Miss Pond stood with her arms akimbo contemplating Dar. Then, she dropped her arms and walked past Dar to the farthest corner of the gym. She removed a lanyard full of keys from around her neck and proceeded to unlock a closet door that had been recessed into the gym wall.

"We're going to do yoga today," she said to Dar. "Since you're here early, I could use your help with the set-up."

Dar hopped up immediately. *Yes, yes, yes!* she thought. If Miss Pond hadn't been watching, Dar would have fist pumped the air. She couldn't have asked for a better p.e. activity for the day.

Dar helped Miss Pond pull out twenty-one yoga mats and place them around the room. Then Miss Pond produced a cell phone and a speaker. She scrolled through some play lists and finally found the one she wanted. She connected the phone to the speaker. Soothing, free-form music filled the gym.

With set-up complete, Dar walked over to the yoga mat in the farthest corner of the gymnasium. She was as far away from the gym entrance as she could possibly be. She lay down flat on her back and closed her eyes.

As she lay there, she could hear the opening and closing of the gym doors. Twenty girls entered in clumps and spurts. She heard their explosive laughter and boisterous outbursts quickly morph into hushed tones as a wall of music hit their ears. Miss Pond was standing by the doors directing everyone to find a mat.

Dar smiled to herself. There would be no interpersonal interactions in this p.e. class, no looking another girl in the eye as she slammed a volleyball down your throat or stole a basketball away from you.

The bell rang to signal the start of E period. "Take a deep breath. Exhale," Miss Pond told the class in her best sing-songy voice.

"Now, come to a seated position. Sit up, girls," she added so that no one would be confused by the phrase "seated position."

There was a quiet rustling as the class sat up. Dar sat up too. She caught sight of Julie, Ariel, and Danni off to her left, each sitting on their own mats. They were far enough away that Dar would have no trouble avoiding them. Secure in the knowledge that she would be safe, at least for the duration of the period, Dar turned her attention back to Miss Pond.

Miss Pond gave an explanation of the principles and practices of yoga. Then, she led the class through a series of stretches, exercises, and postures for thirty minutes. Dar followed each of Miss Pond's movements dutifully, but she could not help but be conscious of the fact that Julie, Ariel, and Danni were only yards away from her. Still, the deep breathing and yoga postures did help her relax somewhat.

Five minutes before the end of class, Miss Pond asked them all to lie flat on their backs and breathe deeply. Dar closed her eyes again. She felt her body tingling all over from the stretches. It felt good.

Miss Pond gently instructed the girls to get up slowly and head to the locker room to get dressed. P.E. was over.

Dar continued to lay still with her eyes closed, ignoring Miss Pond's directions. She waited until everyone else had left and the room was quiet again. Then, she slowly opened her eyes and sat up.

She saw Miss Pond putting the yoga mats back into the closet. She offered to help her. Miss Pond looked quizzically at Dar, but agreed to the help.

"I don't want you to be late for your next class, Darlene," she said.

"I won't be late," Dar lied.

*I might be late,* she thought. *But it doesn't matter to me. It would be worth it to not run into the G Girls.*

She finished helping Miss Pond get the yoga mats into the closet. Then, she headed to the locker room. She cautiously opened the door and peeked inside. The last few students were just clearing out. Julie, Ariel, and Danni were nowhere to be seen.

Dar hurriedly got dressed and scurried on to her math class. She squeezed through the door just as Mr. Reed was pulling it closed and made a beeline for her seat.

"Close one," Robert whispered to her as she sat down. She responded with a little smile in his direction but said nothing.

Dar only half-listened during math class. The day was almost over. One last class to get through, and then she was done for the week, free until Monday.

*What am I going to do this weekend?* she pondered.

She had nothing planned except studying with Elyse. She had nothing to do after school that day. And she had forgotten to text her mother for a ride home. That was just as well since she really did not want to be picked up by her mother for the third time that week.

By the time the bell rang signaling the end of the school day, Dar had made a decision. She was going to walk home. It was just a forty-minute walk, and it was a nice enough day. She did not need to take much with her. She had a backpack in her locker that she could use. She could trade her slip-ons for her cross-trainers and look like a dweeb just this once.

Dar headed to her locker. She loaded her backpack with what she needed. Then she went to the girls' locker room and got her cross-trainers. She switched shoes, placing her slip-ons in her backpack on top of her books. She picked up the backpack and swung it over her shoulders. *It isn't too heavy to carry,* she thought.

Dar reached the main entrance and exited the building. The sun and fresh air hit her face all at once as she accessed the outside world. The weather had been beautiful all week. She made her way down the stairs and through the DHS parking lot. She headed for the sidewalk that led away from the school.

Midway through the parking lot, she intuitively turned around to look back at the building. There, at the top of the stairs, were Julie, Ariel, Danni, and Sean. They were all leaving the school together. She could see the girls laughing and talking, with Sean kind of sauntering along by Julie's side.

*He's feeling ignored, I would say,* Dar thought. *Maybe outnumbered by the girls?* she postulated.

She was surprised to find that she felt a tinge of affection for Sean. She thought back over all their prior interactions however brief, and realized that he had always been kind to her and funny.

She looked again. *They must be heading to Julie's house,* she surmised.

And for the first time that day, Dar felt a longing to be with them. To be leaving school together on a Friday with all the unknown possibilities for fun and excitement over the weekend. To just chill out, watch movies, order a pizza, and hang out late into the night after a long school week. It wasn't too late. She could go back and apologize to Julie. Julie hadn't wanted their friendship to end any more than she had. Julie would accept her apology, no question.

*That's where I belong*, she thought. *I can't go through the rest of the year avoiding them every day. And if I'm not a G Girl, then who am I?*

She tried to think of who else she could hang with. Sure, she knew lots of kids – Brit, Elyse, Robert, Kristen, Damon, and even poor Carrie - but could she really see herself fitting in with any of them?

*Be strong*, she thought. *Be strong. You have a plan. Your plan is to walk home today. That's your plan.*

She turned around and sighed. She began to walk again with her head slightly down. She wanted to rally, but the truth was she felt a little dejected. She hoped that she was doing the right thing.

Dar entered the tree-lined sidewalk. It was covered with red, gold, and brown leaves. She studied the leaves suspiciously as she walked.

*There could be anything underneath those leaves,* she thought. *I could trip over a rock or step in dog poop.*

She was focused on each step when suddenly, she felt someone gently grab a handful of her hair. She wheeled around, wildly swinging the rather large backpack she was carrying on her back. Dar turned around just fast enough to catch sight of Marc jumping out of the way.

"Marc!" Dar's face went from shock to grin.

"Hey," he said laughingly. "You don't have to be so violent. Where are you going, anyway?

"I . . . I'm walking home," Dar stammered awkwardly.

"Can I walk with you?" Marc asked.

"Sure," she said. She had forgotten just how awesome he was.

"Let me carry your backpack," he offered gallantly.

Dar slid the backpack off her shoulders and handed it to Marc. They turned and started to walk.

"I've been looking for you all week," he said, her backpack slung over his shoulder. "Do you want to do something this weekend? Maybe a movie? Stale, fake-buttered popcorn and a 16 oz. Gulpie, how can you say 'no' to that?"

Dar winced. She thought of Marc and Julie seeing a movie together earlier in the week.

"As long as we don't see *Dark Matter*," she said with a dig.

Marc looked slightly bewildered. "I saw that with Julie earlier this week, so no, definitely not," he said cluelessly.

Dar eyed Marc steadily.

*He doesn't know*, she thought. *He doesn't know that Julie and I are no longer friends. He doesn't know that I am no longer a part of her squad, that I am not a G Girl. Should I tell him? He's going to find out eventually. I wonder if it will make any difference to* him? Maybe he won't want to hang with me? Maybe he only likes me because he thinks I am part of Julie's entourage. Or maybe it won't matter. Maybe he doesn't care. Maybe . . .

"Hey," Marc interrupted her thoughts. "Exactly how far away do you live, anyway? This backpack is kind of heavy."

Dar smiled.

# SATURDAY EVENING
## CHAPTER 8

"I miss Dar," Danni blurted out. She had been holding back from expressing her feelings all day long. She could keep them in no longer.

"I miss her too," Ariel said. "Are you ever going to call her?"

Julie tightened her jaw. "That's up to Dar," she replied coldly.

It was Saturday evening. Danni, Ariel, and Julie had spent the entire weekend together. Friday night, they hung out with Sean and watched movies. Saturday afternoon, they went for a hike with Drew and Jeff in their local state park.

On the way back from the park, they decided to cook dinner together. They persuaded Jeff to stop at a nearby grocery store for the ingredients. Back at Julie's house, they made homemade salsa, guacamole, and veggie tacos, accompanied by virgin margaritas. They set the table, posed for selfies, and then ate dinner.

It was now 7:00 p.m. They sat facing each other around Julie's dining room table, nursing their margaritas. The rest of the evening lay before them. They had no plans.

"We drove by Dar yesterday. She was walking away from school. Did you see her?" Ariel asked. "She was with Marc."

"She's seeing Marc again tonight," Danni added.

"Who told you that?" Julie snapped. "Have you been in touch with her?"

"Yes," Danni said defiantly. "I texted her. I wanted to see how she was doing."

"What did she say?" Julie asked suspiciously.

"Nothing about you. She is on a high because Marc asked her out tonight. We didn't talk about our situation at all." Danni made a circular gesture with her hand indicating the three of them.

"Tell us again why she's so mad at you?" Ariel asked. "What happened?"

Julie rose and went to the refrigerator to get some ice. "She thinks I started the rumor about her and Sean," she called from across the room.

"Why does she think that?" Danni asked, scowling.

Julie returned to the table.

"I don't know. Jealously?" she suggested carelessly.

"Jealousy? That doesn't make any sense," Danni

pondered.

"I mean, she thinks that I am jealous of her and Marc, so I started the rumor," Julie explained.

"Jealousy is a terrible feeling. I am jealous of my older sister, Bethany," Ariel confessed.

Julie and Danni both looked at Ariel in astonishment.

"You're jealous of Bethany? Why?" Danni asked.

"No offense to your sister, but you have so much more going on than she does," Julie added.

"I would like to be as smart as she is. She's very smart," Ariel explained.

"She's smart because she spends all of her time studying. She has no life," Julie pointed out.

"My parents are very proud of her. They are always bragging on her. It makes me feel like I'm a nothing," Ariel revealed.

"What? Again, no offense to your sister, but you are one of the hottest girls at DHS. And, you have a much better personality than she does," Julie told her.

"She's shy," Ariel explained.

"Then maybe your parents brag on her because they want to build up her confidence," Julie suggested.

"Your mother adores you," Danni added. "You two are like sisters. I bet she has more fun with you than she does with Bethany. Besides, that's just how parents are. They are always bragging to each other about their kids. Haven't you ever noticed? They are always competing with each other when it comes to their kids' accomplishments. I think it makes them feel like they are being good parents. They think that if they put down other people's kids, their own kids will feel loved and supported."

"My parents do that," Julie said. "My mother will never say anything nice about anyone else's kid."

"But it's not just that," Ariel continued. "I would like to have the experience of school coming easily to me. Or have a special talent the way Julie does."

"I'm shook," Julie responded. "I never thought you cared about any of that."

"Well, I do," Ariel said.

"You always seem so strong in who you are," Danni observed. "I always admired that about you."

"Well, I'm not," Ariel confessed. "At least not in the way you think I am."

"But if you spent all your time studying like Bethany does, would you be happy?" Julie asked.

Ariel considered for a moment. "Even if I did, I don't think it would make any difference. I'm just not that smart."

Danni and Julie were silent. They wanted to tell Ariel that she was wrong, that she could achieve high grades like Bethany, that she was smart enough, however, they just weren't sure if that were true.

"See, this is why we need Dar," Danni said, "She

would know what to say to make you feel better."

"Ariel, you are only 15. Maybe you just haven't found your thing, the thing that you are going to be good at in life," Julie suggested.

"I don't know . . . maybe," Ariel responded. "Jealousy is horrible because it's hard to change. You can get over feeling sad or angry, but jealousy is based on how you feel about yourself," Ariel observed. "Nothing makes you feel better. Nothing makes it go away."

"That's not true," Julie asserted. "When I feel jealous, I get angry. And then I have to do something about it."

"Like what? Bethany is my sister. I'm not going to do anything to hurt her."

"We could always quietly judge her behind her back," Julie said, only half joking.

"You have better hair than she does," Danni added as if to demonstrate.

Ariel abruptly changed the subject. "So, what are we going to do about Dar?" she asked. "We have to make this right."

Julie hesitated. "Okay. I'll call her in the morning," she relented.

# SUNDAY
## CHAPTER 9

On Sunday morning, Dar awoke to the text alert sound on her phone - *ting, ting!* She opened her eyes, reached for her phone and drew it to her. There were a bevy of texts awaiting her attention. She rolled over and sat up. The first three were from Marc. She quickly opened the phone and read them.

The first one said, "Barnsy says yes."

Dar laughed. It was a private joke between them.

The second one said, "The gibbons want to know where you are?" Also a private joke.

And the third one just said, "WAKE UP!!!" with a menacing close-up of a rooster's eye.

Dar wanted to text Marc back right away, but her attention was drawn to the next set of texts. There was one from Danni asking about her night with Marc. There was one from Ariel that said, "What's going on? Call me." And lastly, there was one from Julie. It just said, "I need to talk to you."

Dar was surprised. She hadn't expected to hear from any of them, let alone all three. She wondered what the three of them had done all weekend without her. What did Julie tell them about why she wasn't there? It was a bit alarming to have all three of them wanting to talk to her at once. They must have had quite a conversation about her for the three of them to be contacting her so early in the morning.

Dar put down the phone. She stared off into space. She had left school on Friday prepared to face one of the most difficult weekends of her life. Instead, it was turning out to be one of the best. Not only did Marc walk her home on Friday, he invited himself in, met her family, charmed her mother, and hung out with her until dinner time.

They made plans to see a movie on Saturday. So, instead of missing Julie, Ariel, and Danni all weekend, she spent Friday night and all day Saturday excited about seeing Marc. Between meeting with Elyse on Saturday afternoon and seeing Marc on Saturday evening, she did not even have time to think about what she might be missing with her friends.

Then, last night was a fantasy come true. Marc picked her up with his parents' car. She did not even know he had his license. They saw an early movie and then went back to his house. They hung out and watched TV until about 11:00 p.m. Then, he drove her home.

Now that Dar was sure Marc liked her, she found herself relaxing around him more and more. They were quickly becoming close. Did he kiss her? Of course! And kissed her and kissed her and kissed her.

Dar sighed. She had planned to spend her day finishing up her homework, eating dinner with her family, and maybe seeing Marc again in the late afternoon, if her parents allowed it. Confronting her former friends had not been part of her plans.

Dar got out of bed. She headed for the shower. She needed to figure out what she wanted to do. She really didn't want to deal with Julie or Ariel today, but she wasn't going to cower from them either.

She decided that she would begin by answering Danni's text. That would be easy. Danni had been texting her all weekend anyway, and Dar had responded as if everything were normal between them. They had both judiciously skirted the subject of Dar's withdrawal from their group. Dar appreciated the subtle way in which Danni let her know that nothing had changed between them, despite the complexity of their situation. She decided that she would probe Danni for more information before stepping into any mine fields where Julie and Ariel were concerned.

Dar exited the shower. She threw on a thick, fluffy robe and went to find her phone. Her fingers hovered over the keyboard as she considered what to say.

"Last night was good," she texted.

"What did you do?" Danni returned.

"A movie and his house afterwards," Dar informed

her.

"Netflix and chill already?" Danni asked.

"It wasn't like that," Dar answered.

Danni responded with a series of suggestive emoji stickers.

"None of the above," Dar replied flatly. She quickly changed the subject.

"Julie and Ariel texted me this morning," Dar wrote.

Within seconds, her phone was ringing. It was Danni.

"That was a quick response. You must really want to talk about them," Dar answered, slightly amused.

"What did they say?" Danni asked, launching right into it.

"Hmmm, let's see," Dar drawled. "Ariel wants me to call her, and Julie wants to talk to me. Got any idea why?" She asked with more than a hint of sarcasm in her voice. Her tone went right by Danni, however.

"Isn't it obvious? Our situation," Danni responded.

"I have no problem with you or Ariel. It's Julie who _ "

"Dar, the Sean rumor wasn't Julie's fault," Danni interrupted her.

"I never said it was," Dar answered, a bit perplexed.

"But isn't that why you won't hang with us?" Danni asked.

"No. Is that what Julie told you?" *She's*

*unbelievable!* Dar thought.

"Why are you so mad at us, then?" Danni asked.

"I'm not mad at any of you. Julie is not talking to me," Dar answered.

"What? Why?" Danni prodded.

"You'll have to ask Julie that," Dar responded.

There was a moment of befuddled silence.

"That's not what Julie thinks," Danni said finally. "She thinks you're mad at her because you think she started the Sean rumor.

*Yeah, right she does,* Dar thought.

"We have to talk about this all together," Danni continued. "Ariel and I want you back. This isn't right. You should have been hanging with us all weekend."

*Well!* Dar mused. *I wonder what Julie thinks of that? Her minions are not following her orders. That must suck for her. No wonder she wants to talk to me.*

"My parents are calling me to leave for church," Danni informed her. "I'll call you when I get back."

"Sure," Dar agreed.

Danni hung up.

Dar sat motionless on her bed, contemplating what to do next. *Should I call Ariel or answer Julie?* she pondered.

She stared at the phone as if the solution were about to spring forth from its depths. Finally, on impulse, she decided to return Julie's text.

"Okay," she wrote, agreeing to talk with her. Dar waited to see if she would get a response. A few seconds later a reply appeared.

"Java at 3:00?" Julie proposed.

"K," she confirmed. The communication ended there.

△△△

Dar dried her hair and got dressed. She headed downstairs to hunt for something to eat. She was well aware that she still had not answered Marc's texts. The intrusion of her friends and their problems into her day had broken his spell over her.

She entered the kitchen. Her father was at the stove cooking pancakes. Her mother was sitting at the table with a cup of coffee stationed in front of her. Her sisters were there too, each one with a plate full of pancakes; both of them looking very sticky, and both talking more than eating. Her mother was listening to them with an amused expression on her face.

Dar went to the refrigerator. She took out the orange juice and poured herself a glass. She brought it to the table and sat down next to her mother.

"Dar, do you want some pancakes?" Her father asked.

"Sure," she replied.

She sat quietly for a while, observing the scene and listening to her sisters prattling on. Finally she asked, "Mom, can I get a ride to meet Julie at 3:00?"

Her mother thought for a moment. "I don't see why not," she answered. "Your sisters are playing soccer this afternoon, but we will be back by 2:00 – 2:30. Do you want to come?"

"No, I want to finish my homework before I go out," Dar replied.

"Sounds reasonable," her mother responded. "What time will you be back?"

"Probably around 5:00," Dar answered. "I'll text if I need a ride."

△△△

Dar quietly consumed her pancakes and returned to her room. She wanted to answer Marc's texts before she did anything else. She reread his three texts.

"You are always waking me up," she wrote, referring to both his last text and the very first time they met.

"You are always falling asleep," came Marc's reply.

"I didn't fall asleep last night," Dar said.

"True," Marc responded. "I would have taken that personally," he added.

"I had to see the end of the movie, didn't I?" she

teased.

"Was that the only reason?" Marc asked.

"No, not the only reason," she answered.

"Will you be awake later this afternoon?" Marc asked.

"I will definitely be awake later this afternoon. I am meeting with Julie," Dar responded.

Marc sent an emoji frowny face.

"Will you be awake after you meet with Julie?" he asked.

"I think so," Dar returned.

"If not, I am going to wake you up," Marc warned her.

"You promise?" she asked.

"Yes," he answered.

## △△△

Content with Marc's assurance that he would contact her later, Dar got ready to complete her homework assignments. She had already done most of them, but there were still a few unfinished algebra problems, and she wanted to do one last review before her Spanish test. It was about an hour's worth of work, and then she would be free to relax for the rest of the day. She took out her study materials, got organized, and began to focus.

Dar finished her algebra problems easily. She

checked the time. It was almost noon. She would probably be done before 1:00 p.m. By then, Danni would be home.

Dar worked her way through the vocabulary and grammar for her Spanish test. The review was going quickly. She and Elyse had already done a good job of learning the material, so it was just a matter of jogging her memory.

She was three quarters of the way through the review now. She half expected Danni to call back and interrupt her while she was studying, but so far, Danni hadn't. What more did Danni have to say anyway?

Ariel and Danni did not know the real reason why she and Julie were fighting. They thought it was because Dar blamed Julie for the Sean rumor. What was it Danni had said? "The Sean rumor wasn't Julie's fault." That's what she had said.

Dar had no intention of telling either of them what really happened. She just wanted to find out if Danni knew why Julie wanted to talk. Danni probably wouldn't be aware of Julie's real motives. However, Dar thought she might be able to pick up a few clues from talking with Danni.

Dar finished studying. She scooped up her study materials and stowed them away in her backpack. She phoned Danni immediately.

"I was just about to call you," Danni said upon answering the phone.

"Are you back home now?" Dar asked.

"Yes, I'm home. Ariel is with me. I'm putting you on speaker," Danni told her.

"Hey Dar," Ariel yelled from the background.

"Ariel is with you?" Dar asked, a little surprised. "What are you two doing?"

"We're studying," Danni informed her.

"You and Ariel are studying?" Dar asked with more incredulity than she had intended.

"Yes. Long story," Danni said. "Did you talk with Julie yet?"

"No, not yet. We're getting together later. Do you know what she wants to talk to me about - other than to tell me that the Sean rumor was not her fault?" Dar asked.

"Dar, about the Sean rumor, what I meant was - ," Danni started.

"Let me talk to her," Ariel interrupted, stretching out her hand to take Danni's phone.

"Ariel wants to talk to you," Danni said. She handed the phone to Ariel.

"Dar, I have something to tell you. Promise me you won't be mad?" Ariel started.

Dar instantly felt her body tense up. Something in Ariel's voice made her stomach flip. She braced herself as if for bad news.

"I can't promise that, Ariel, not until I hear what you have to say," Dar replied, unmoved.

"Okay. Well, the Sean rumor wasn't Julie's fault, or rather, it wasn't *just* Julie's fault. Actually, it really wasn't anybody's fault," Ariel began.

"The thing is . . . Julie and I started the rumor . . . but . . . it was just by accident. We really didn't mean to," Ariel confessed.

"What?" Dar could barely take in the words.

"Julie and I were pranking Sean in the hallway at school. We were teasing him about taking you home, and someone must have overheard us. And then, the rumor spread so fast. Within an hour we were getting texts about you. We couldn't stop it."

"WTF, Ariel! Did you even try?" Dar asked angrily.

"Honestly Dar, we didn't think it was such a big deal. But then you got so upset; we were afraid to tell you what happened. We didn't even tell Danni until this morning. We thought the rumor would just fade away after a while. And . . . it did. No one even talks about you and Sean anymore."

"Ariel, my life has been a living hell since Tuesday!" Dar said accusingly.

"I know. I'm sorry. But really, we didn't mean for this to happen."

"I can't believe you didn't tell me this sooner," Dar said. She was reeling from the revelation.

"I know. I suck as a friend. I'm so sorry!" Ariel apologized.

Dar did not respond. What could she say? *I forgive*

*you? I don't forgive you?* Neither one matched the complexity of how she felt.

Danni took the phone back. "Dar, we really miss you. We're not the *G Girls* without you!" she said.

"We're the *G Minus Girls* without you!" Ariel yelled from the background.

"Yes, we're the *G Minus Girls* without you!" Danni echoed.

Dar remained silent.

Finally, she asked, "Does Julie know you're telling me this?"

"Yes. We agreed. We agreed yesterday that we would tell you. Julie said she would call you this morning, and she did. I mean, she texted you," Ariel explained.

"Dar, earlier you said that Julie wasn't speaking to you? Could you be wrong? Maybe you both misunderstood each other," Danni suggested gently.

"No, Danni. I am not wrong," Dar said.

"Are you sure?" Danni asked.

"Yes. I'm sure," Dar answered.

"What time are you meeting Julie? We'll come too," Danni offered.

"Thanks, but no," Dar said firmly. "This is between Julie and me."

△△△

Dar hung up the phone. She instantly collapsed onto her bed. Her body felt heavy, slammed with the truth and burdened by betrayal, depression, and grief. The tears welled up in her eyes and would not stop coming, even as she tried to hold them back. She cried uncontrollably.

She had shown great courage and great strength throughout one of the most difficult weeks of her life. She had been determined not to let the events of the week devastate her, and she had been successful up until now. But the revelation that the friends she loved had kept this secret from her was more than she could bear.

She lay on her bed, immobilized. The tears kept coming and coming. The very friends to whom she would normally turn for comfort were now the source of bitter pain. There was no one else. She felt so alone. She cried and cried.

The tears began to subside now with only one or two escaping here and there. She felt drained. Her mind was foggy; her head ached. She longed to go to sleep. She teetered on the edge of consciousness, trying to decide whether to allow herself to take the plunge. Her family would be back in half an hour. Exhaustion beckoned. She thought of Marc's joke about how she was always falling asleep. She faintly smiled inwardly. Outwardly, she did not move a muscle. She surrendered to the darkness.

$$\triangle\triangle\triangle$$

"Dar. . . Dar. . .."

She heard her name far off in the distance.

"Dar, do you still want a ride?" Her mother asked.

*No*, she thought.

"We should leave in about ten minutes," her mother added.

Dar opened her eyes. She mechanically sat up. The room was spinning. She felt for the floor against her feet. It was there. She looked down at her pretty, pink toenail polish and was reassured. She stood up and headed for the bathroom. Once there, she looked at herself in the mirror. Her eye make-up was a mess from crying; her hair disheveled.

Dar washed her face, lifting up her hair, and splashing water around the back of her neck. She wiped the blotchy eye make-up from around her eyes and reapplied eyeliner and mascara. She did her best to rein in the frizzy and wayward strands of her hair. She studied her image to see if it was presentable. It was good enough.

Dar returned to her room. She grabbed her phone and a small purse and headed downstairs.

"Dar! Dar! We won!" Her youngest sister, Carly,

came running towards her.

"Nice," she responded, offering her sister a hand to slap. Having received her reward, Carly abruptly turned around and walked off.

"I'll be in the car," she told her mother.

"I'll be there in a minute," her mother replied.

ΔΔΔ

Dar entered Java at 2:45 p.m. She scanned the room. Julie had not yet arrived. She ordered a large passionfruit iced tea and sat down at a table facing the door so that Julie could see her.

Dar did not have a plan for what she was going to say. All she knew was that she was furious and hurt. She doubted there was anything Julie could do to fix the situation, but Dar had already agreed to meet her, so Julie had one last chance.

At 2:55 p.m., the door opened. Julie walked in. She saw Dar immediately and came straight to her table. She sat down across from Dar. They studied each other in silence, each one waiting for the other to speak. Finally, Julie said, "I talked to Danni and Ariel a little while ago. They let me know they told you how the Sean rumor got started."

In a hushed voice, barely a whisper, Dar replied, "Ariel and Danni think the Sean rumor was an accident. But I know what you did to Carrie Ellis. I know how you operate. Someone in the hallway accidentally overheard you pranking Sean? How did that happen? The same way Teresa Manning accidentally overheard you talking about Carrie Ellis?'"

Dar stared at Julie. "I can barely look at you right now. How could you do that to me? You just had to stop me and Marc from happening. Why? Why would you do that to me?"

Julie took a deep breath and spoke slowly. "Honestly? I saw you and Marc connecting and - "

"And you just couldn't stand to see anyone else getting the attention," Dar interrupted her.

"No, it wasn't that. It wasn't that at all," Julie corrected her. "You and I have always been so close. I . . . I guess I got scared . . . scared I was going to lose . . . .." Julie stopped short of finishing her sentence.

"Control! You were going to say 'lose control' over me, weren't you?" Dar accused her.

"No! I was going to say, 'scared I was going to lose you as a friend,'" Julie finally spit out.

"Julie!" In a split second, Dar's anger turned to confusion. "How could you think that about me after all this time? Besides, you were the one who stopped talking to me. You were the one who gave me the ultimatum."

"When I gave you the ultimatum, I never thought that you would choose to walk away from me," Julie said.

"You wouldn't talk to me. What did you expect me to do?" Dar reminded her.

"I thought you would be on my side. It was a test of our friendship, and you chose someone else over me." Julie's lower lip began to quiver.

"I did choose someone else over you. I chose myself," Dar told her. "I have been trying to explain this to you. I have to be able to make my own decisions and exercise my own judgement in our friendship. I have to be able to tell you when I think something is right or wrong.

"Julie, you can't go through life trying to control everyone and taking revenge when they don't obey you. That's not going to work. Control is not the same as friendship."

"It makes me feel better," Julie said with a shrug.

"Seriously? Does this really feel better? Are you having a good time? Cause I'm not," Dar said angrily.

Julie bit her lower lip.

Dar continued. "Besides, how could you think so little of me that you think I would abandon my friends because I had a boyfriend?

"And how can you think so little of yourself that you think you have to control your friends, or you won't have any?" Dar asked. "Control is not love, Julie."

Julie dropped her head as if she had been punched. Her hair fell forward and covered her face.

She looked down at the table. Her eyes filled with tears.

Dar continued. "I don't know what's going to happen between me and Marc. I like him a lot. I'm going to be spending more time with him. Things are going to change for us, Julie. We are going to change. You can't stop that. How are we going to stay friends if I can't be honest with you? How are we going to stay friends if you are going to play games with me?

"Friendship is not just about your squad ranking, Julie. It's not a game. If you make it a game, you will lose," Dar said threateningly.

"The real question is, do you want an equal friendship, or do you want to dominate me? Because if you want to dominate me, I'm out."

Julie was now crying. The tears flowed from her eyes. She tried to wipe them away with her hand. Dar got up and went to the condiment bar. She returned with a stack of napkins. She gently placed them in front of Julie who selected one and attempted to dab her eyes. Neither one spoke.

Dar waited patiently for Julie to collect herself. She had said all she wanted to say, all she needed to say. She calmly waited for Julie to respond.

*"Daaarrr!"*

Their intimate silence was shattered by the voices of Danni and Ariel. Danni circled the table to give Dar a hug. Ariel followed.

"We're so glad you're here!" Ariel exclaimed.

Dar looked at the two of them in dismay. She had asked them not to come, and instead, they showed up at the worst possible moment.

Danni grabbed a chair and sat down.

"So? Are we the *G Girls* again?" she asked, looking from Dar to Julie and back again. Danni suddenly noticed Julie's face. "Is everything okay?" she asked anxiously.

No one spoke. Julie looked penetratingly at Dar. Finally, she said, "Yes, we are the *G Girls* again."

"Woohooo! Let's celebrate!" Ariel said. "Do you want to get a pizza? I'm starving from studying!"

Julie laughed at her.

"I can't. My mother is coming to get me at 5:00," Dar fibbed a little.

"Oh Dar, we haven't seen you all weekend," Ariel said. "Ask your mother if you can stay out for a few more hours."

Dar hesitated. The truth was, she really didn't want to. Yes, her friends were reaching out to her. Yes, they were showing her love. Yes, they wanted her back in their group. Yet some uneasiness remained for her, some residual anger towards them, some hurt.

Something had changed in the way she felt about each one of them. What was it? Why was she still feeling uncomfortable? *Trust! It was trust!* Their bonds of trust had been broken, and it was going to take more than just words to rebuild those bonds. She wondered if she would ever be able to truly trust them again, the way she used to. Only time would tell.

# MONDAY MORNING
## CHAPTER 10

"Dar, are you coming?" her father yelled up the stairs.

"Yes," she yelled back.

Dar quickly grabbed her backpack and headed downstairs. For the last ten minutes, she had been sitting on her bed texting with Marc. The texting continued during the short car ride to school.

They had started communicating yesterday, after Dar returned home from meeting with Julie. They continued until just before Dar fell asleep.

They tried to figure out how they could see each other during the school day. They compared their schedules and discovered that their paths never crossed. Marc ate first lunch, and she ate second. They had different recesses and different study halls. They made a plan to meet just outside the entrance to DHS before school started.

Mr. Blaise had no sooner pulled the car into the school drop-off area when Dar spotted Marc. He was on the landing outside the entrance to DHS, sitting on a half-wall, studying his phone. Dar exited the car with a quick goodbye to her dad. She climbed the stairs with her heart pounding. Marc caught sight of her just as she was nearing the top step.

"Get over here," he said playfully, extending his arm to her.

"You're a very bossy person," Dar responded, even as she obeyed him. They entered the school building together, holding hands.

"Which way do you go now?" Marc asked.

"Mr. Clark's room," she told him.

"I'll walk you there," Marc said.

They arrived at her classroom. Julie was already inside, sitting in her seat. Dar ran in and quickly dropped off her backpack. She gave Julie a little smile as she walked past her. Then, she returned to Marc. The two of them stood together in the hallway ignoring the DHS PDA rules. After a few minutes, Marc left for his class.

"You two are bonding quickly," Julie commented as she watched Dar take her seat.

"He's like a cute, cuddly, puppy dog," Dar said with a toothy grin.

Julie laughed. "A cocker spaniel?" she asked.

"No, more of a beagle," Dar answered.

Julie laughed again.

"I guess you'll be seeing him after school today, then?" Julie inquired.

"Marc did ask me if I wanted to do something later," Dar informed her, "but I told him I was just going to hang with my friends."

Julie smiled.

# QUESTIONS FOR DISCUSSION

1) Do you think Dar and Julie's friendship will last? Do you think the *G Girls* will stay together as a squad?

2) Do you think Julie will be able to change?

3) Do you think Dar is brave? How do you view the choices she made in *The G Girls*?

4) Has a friend ever done anything that you did not think was right? How did you respond?

5) Do you have friends that you do not really trust? How do you handle them?

6) Spreading rumors and slander has become a way of life in America. Do you believe every rumor you hear? Have you ever been the subject of a rumor?

7) Often in books and movies, people are portrayed as good or bad; superhero or villain. Do you think that people really are all good or all bad? Do you think the characters in *The G Girls* are all good or all bad?

8) Do you like Dar? Do you like Julie? Would you be friends with them if they were in your school?

9) Do you compare yourself to other people? How does it make you feel about yourself? How do you deal with jealousy?

10) What else could the "G" stand for in *G Girls*?

11) A literary theme is the main idea or underlying meaning a writer explores in a novel, short story, or other literary work. The theme of a story can be conveyed using characters, setting, dialogue, plot, or a combination of all of these elements. A literary work can have more than one theme. What do you think the themes are in *The G Girls*? What evidence from the novel supports your conclusion?

# GRATITUDE

I would like to express my love and gratitude to all my cherished family and friends, especially my husband, who encouraged me and put up with me during this very long writing project.

I would also like to thank Richard Ayers, Pattie Wesley, and Maryann Hickelton for their editorial feedback and assistance. Without them, this project could not have been completed. I would like to thank Kim Adams and Peter Seltzer for being my early readers, and my parents Louis and Louise Valentine for their financial support.

I would like to express my love and gratitude to all the teenagers who have been part of my life. You are a fun, creative bunch, and your energy has enriched my life greatly!

And finally, I would like to give a special shout-out to my own high school besties who provide me with love and support to this very day.

Thank you to all!

# ABOUT THE AUTHOR

## S J Valentine

S J Valentine has been teaching voice and piano to children and teens of all ages for the past 25 years. This is her first venture into fiction.

www.ingramcontent.com/pod-product-compliance
Lightning Source LLC
Chambersburg PA
CBHW020958180626
46814CB00003B/1156